DK READERS

Level 3

Shark Attack!
Titanic
Invaders from Outer Space
Movie Magic
Plants Bite Back!
Time Traveler
Bermuda Triangle
Tiger Tales
Zeppelin: The Age of the Airship
Spies
Terror on the Amazon
Disasters at Sea
The Story of Anne Frank
Abraham Lincoln: Lawyer, Leader, Legend
George Washington: Soldier, Hero, President
Extreme Sports
Spiders' Secrets
The Big Dinosaur Dig
Space Heroes: Amazing Astronauts
The Story of Chocolate
School Days Around the World
Polar Bear Alert!
Welcome to China
My First Ballet Show
Ape Adventures
Greek Myths
MLB: Home Run Heroes: Big Mac, Sammy, and Junior
MLB: World Series Heroes
MLB: Record Breakers
MLB: Down to the Wire: Baseball's Great Pennant Races
Star Wars: Star Pilot
Star Wars: I Want to Be a Jedi
Star Wars: The Story of Darth Vader
Marvel Heroes: Amazing Powers
The X-Men School
Abraham Lincoln: Abogado, Líder, Leyenda *en español*
Al Espacio: La Carrera a la Luna *en español*
Fantastic Four: The World's Greatest Superteam
Wolverine: Awesome Powers

Level 4

Volcanoes and Other Natural Disasters
Pirates! Raiders of the High Seas
Micro Monsters
Going for Gold!
Extreme Machines
Flying Ace: The Story of Amelia Earhart
Black Beauty
Free at Last! The Story of Martin Luther King, Jr.
Joan of Arc
Spooky Spinechillers
Welcome to The Globe! The Story of Shakespeare's Theater
Space Station: Accident on Mir
Atlantis: The Lost City?
Dinosaur Detectives
Danger on the Mountain: Scaling the World's Highest Peaks
Crime Busters
The Story of Muhammad Ali
First Flight: The Story of the Wright Brothers
D-Day Landings: the Story of the Allied Invasion
Solo Sailing
Thomas Edison: The Great Inventor
Dinosaurs! Battle of the Bones
Skate!
MLB: Strikeout Kings
MLB: Super Shortstops: Jeter, Nomar, and A-Rod
MLB: The Story of the New York Yankees
MLB: The World of Baseball
MLB: October Magic: All the Best World Series!
JLA: Batman's Guide to Crime and Detection
JLA: Superman's Guide to the Universe
JLA: Aquaman's Guide to the Oceans
JLA: Wonder Woman's Book of Myths
JLA: Flash's Guide to Speed
JLA: Green Lantern's Guide to Great Inventions
The Story of the X-Men: How it all Began
Creating the X-Men: How Comic Books Come to Life
Spider-Man's Amazing Powers
The Story of Spider-Man
The Incredible Hulk's Book of Strength
The Story of the Incredible Hulk
Transformers: The Awakening
Transformers: The Quest
Transformers: The Unicron Battles
Transformers: The Uprising
Transformers: Megatron Returns
Transformers: Terracon Attack
Star Wars: Galactic Crisis!
Star Wars: Beware the Dark Side
Star Wars: Epic Battles
Marvel Heroes: Greatest Battles
Fantastic Four: Evil Adversaries
Graphic Readers: The Price of Victory
Graphic Readers: The Terror Trail
Graphic Readers: Curse of the Crocodile God
Graphic Readers: Instruments of Death
Graphic Readers: The Spy-Catcher Gang
Graphic Readers: Wagon Train Adventure
Los Asombrosos Poderes de Spider-Man *en español*
La Historia de Spider-Man *en español*
Star Wars The Clone Wars: Jedi Adventures
Wolverine: The Story of Wolverine
Iron Man: The Rise of Iron Man

LONDON, NEW YORK, MELBOURNE,
MUNICH, AND DELHI

For Dorling Kindersley
Designer Sandra Perry
Senior Editor Laura Gilbert
Design Manager Rob Perry
Managing Editor Catherine Saunders
Art Director Lisa Lanzarini
Publishing Manager Simon Beecroft
Category Publisher Alex Allan
Production Editor Sean Daly
Production Controller Nick Seston

Reading Consultant
Linda B. Gambrell, Ph.D.

First published in the United States in 2010
by DK Publishing
375 Hudson Street,
New York, New York 10014

10 11 12 13 14 10 9 8 7 6 5 4 3 2 1
176237—10/09

DK books are available at special discounts when purchased in bulk
for sales promotions, premiums, fund-raising, or educational use.
For details, contact: DK Publishing Special Markets,
375 Hudson Street, New York, New York 10014
SpecialSales@dk.com

A catalog record for this book is available from the Library of Congress.

ISBN: 978-0-7566-5770-3 (Paperback)
ISBN: 978-0-7566-5771-0 (Hardcover)

Color reproduction by Alta Image, UK
Printed and bound by L-Rex, China

Discover more at

Contents

A Note to Parents

DK READERS is a compelling program for beginning readers, designed in conjunction with leading literacy experts, including Dr. Linda Gambrell, Professor of Education at Clemson University. Dr. Gambrell has served as President of the National Reading Conference and the College Reading Association, and has recently been elected to serve as President of the International Reading Association.

Beautiful illustrations and superb full-color photographs combine with engaging, easy-to-read stories to offer a fresh approach to each subject in the series. Each DK READER is guaranteed to capture a child's interest while developing his or her reading skills, general knowledge, and love of reading.

The five levels of DK READERS are aimed at different reading abilities, enabling you to choose the books that are exactly right for your child:

Pre-level 1: Learning to read
Level 1: Beginning to read
Level 2: Beginning to read alone
Level 3: Reading alone
Level 4: Proficient readers

The "normal" age at which a child begins to read can be anywhere from three to eight years old. Adult participation through the lower levels is very helpful for providing encouragement, discussing storylines, and sounding out unfamiliar words.

No matter which level you select, you can be sure that you are helping your child learn to read, then read to learn!

DK READERS

READING 3 ALONE

THE INVINCIBLE IRON MAN

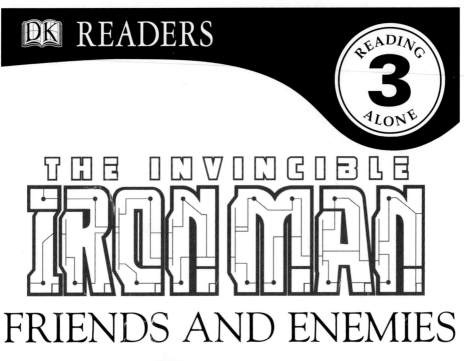

FRIENDS AND ENEMIES

Written by
Michael
Teitelbaum

DK

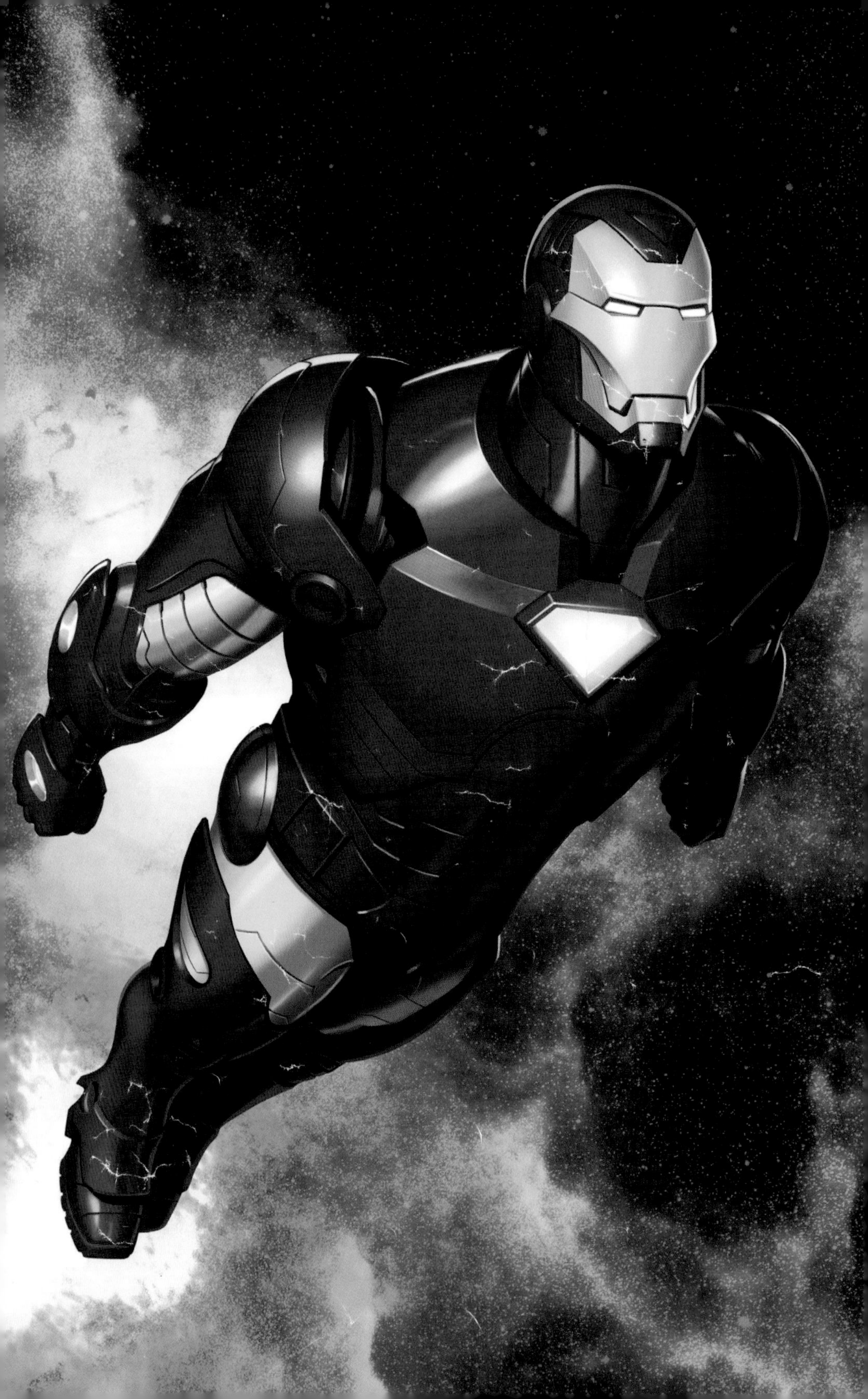

Introduction

Meet Iron Man! He is a Super Hero with superhuman strength. Powered by his jetboots, he soars through the sky in his red and gold suit of armor. The unibeam on Iron Man's chest projects an energy shield and a pinpoint laser, which can cut through practically anything. Repulsor beams in his gloves can blast whatever gets in his way.
But who is Iron Man really?

Iron Man's armor
Iron Man has created many different suits of armor. They include a heavy gray armor, deep-sea armor, space travel armor, and Hulkbuster armor.

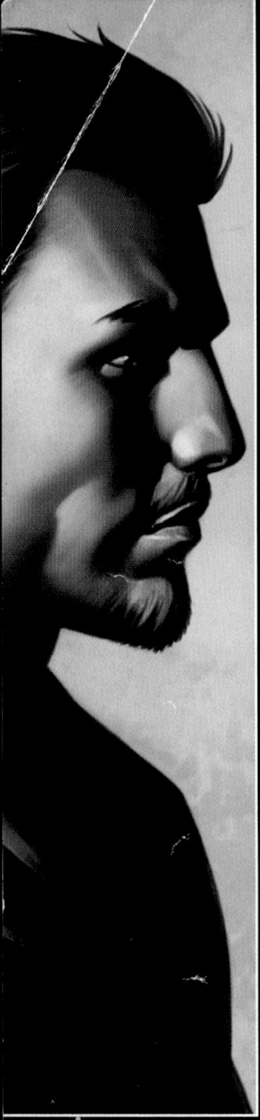

Tony Stark

Beneath his armor, Iron Man is really Tony Stark.

At the age of 15, Tony studied at a top technology college. His parents were killed in a car crash when he was 21, and he inherited Stark Industries from them.

Nowadays, Tony is a weapons manufacturer, scientist, genius inventor, and a billionaire businessman who runs the very successful Stark Industries.

While testing a glider, Tony crashed on an island and was taken prisoner by the evil group A.I.M. (Advanced Idea Mechanics). With scientist Ho Yinsen, Tony built a suit of armor and used it to free himself. Iron Man was born!

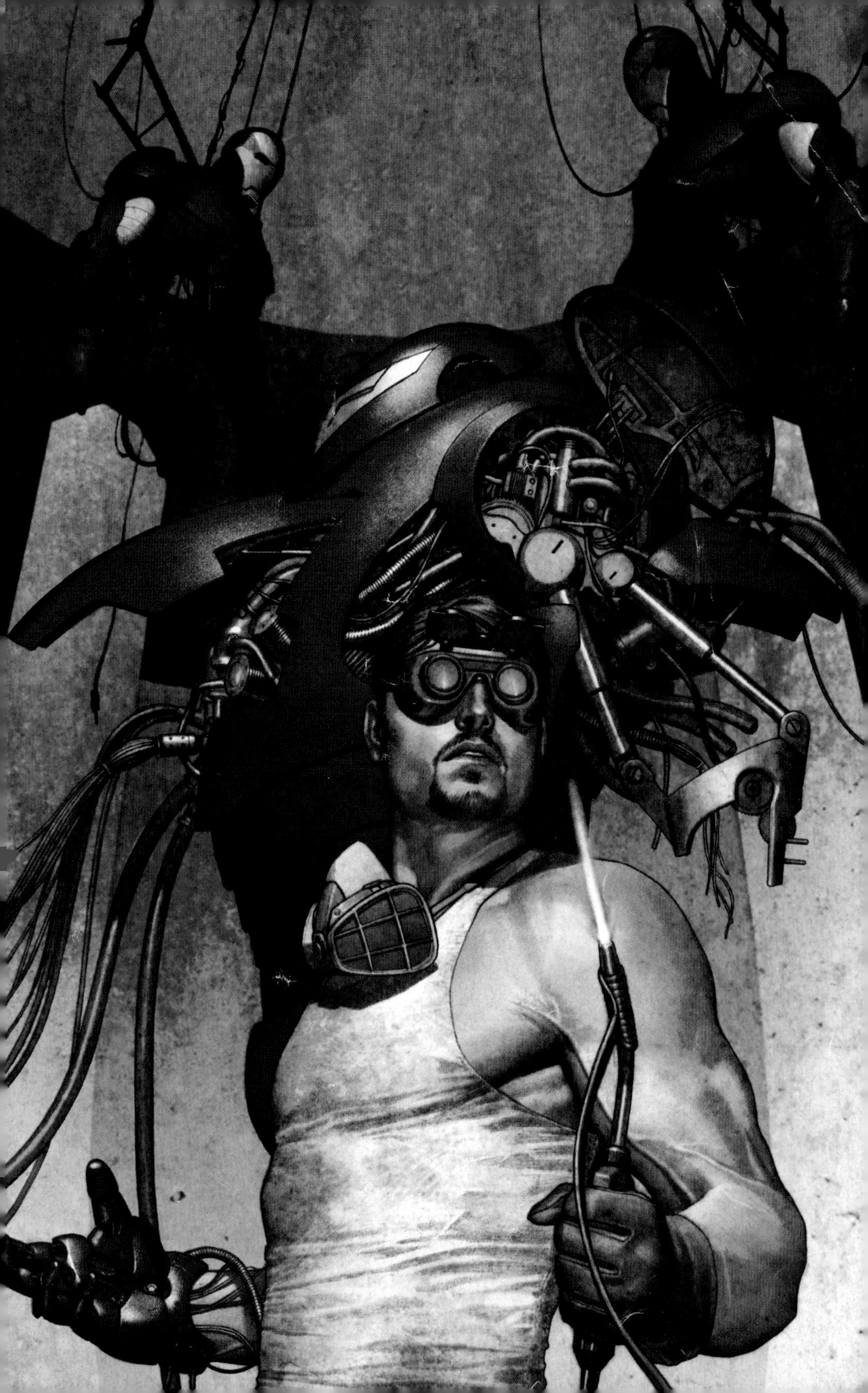

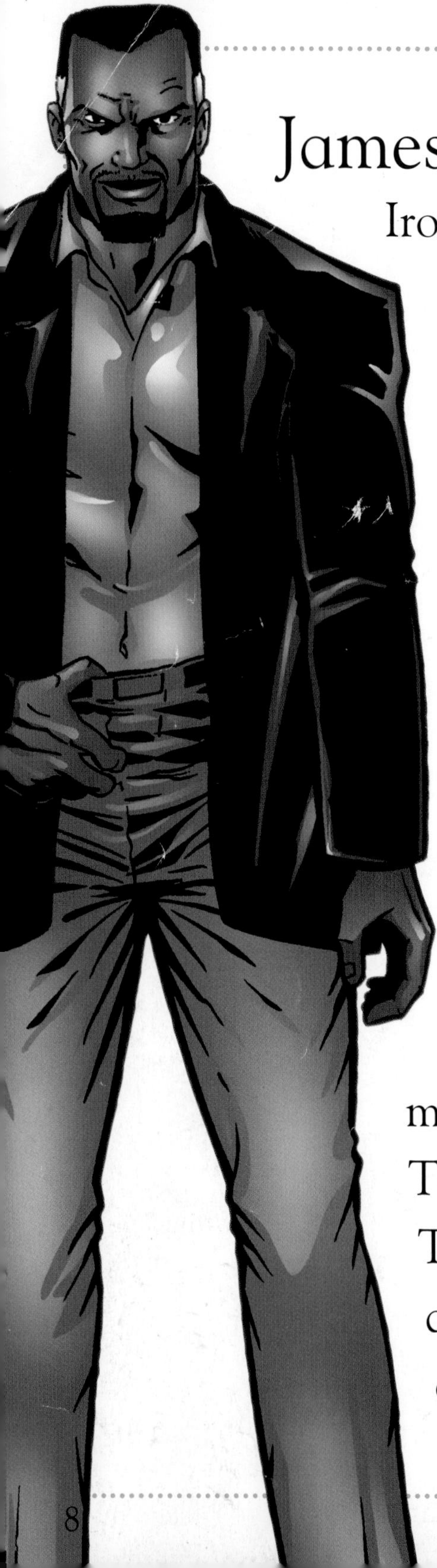

James Rhodes

Iron Man has teamed up with other Super Heroes and fought Super Villains, making both friends and enemies.

James Rhodes is one of Tony's best friends. "Rhodey" was a decorated military pilot. He met Tony when Stark Industries was making weapons.

After Rhodey left the military, he became Tony's pilot. He is one of Tony's trusted associates and Stark Industries' chief aviation officer.

James Rhodes: Iron Man

Tony can always rely on Rhodey. When Iron Man was framed for murder, Rhodey wore Iron Man's armor again and filled in for his friend.

When Tony was forced out of action due to health problems, Rhodey put on Tony's Iron Man armor and took his place. Eventually, Rhodey put on an advanced armor that Tony had built called the Variable Threat Response Battle Suit. He became known as War Machine.

War Machine's combat armor includes a mini-gun on his shoulder.

Virginia "Pepper" Potts

Virginia Potts began working at Stark Industries as a secretary. She got her nickname, "Pepper," because of the freckles on her face. Tony first noticed Pepper Potts when she corrected an accounting mistake he made. He appreciated her talent and loyalty, and made Pepper his executive assistant.

Pepper and Tony began to fall in love.

But they decided to remain just friends and not let their relationship distract them from work.

Pepper eventually learned that Tony was really Iron Man.

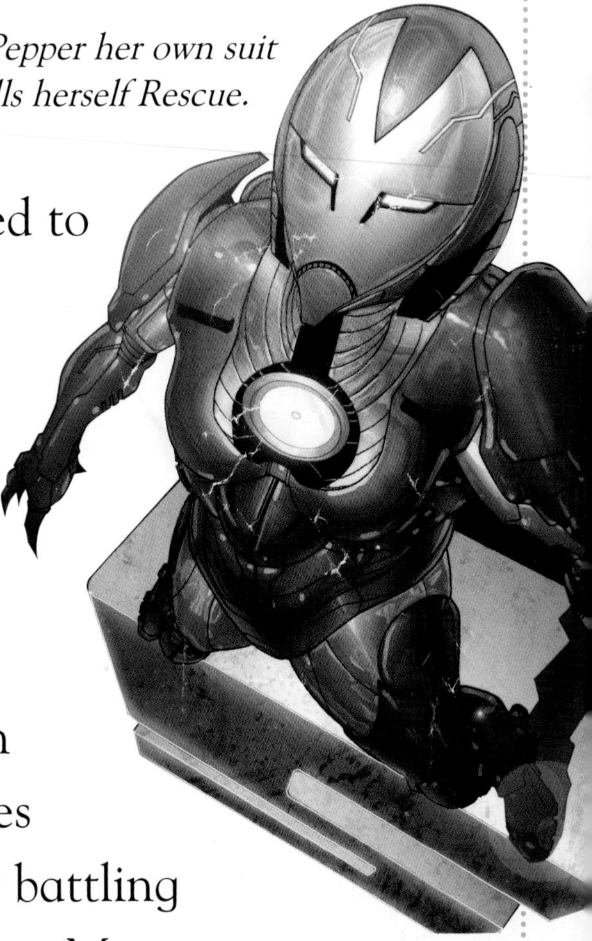

Tony even gave Pepper her own suit of armor. She calls herself Rescue.

However, she helped to keep his secret and often covered for her friend.

Pepper is brilliant at making business decisions. She often runs Stark Industries when Tony is away battling Super Villains as Iron Man.

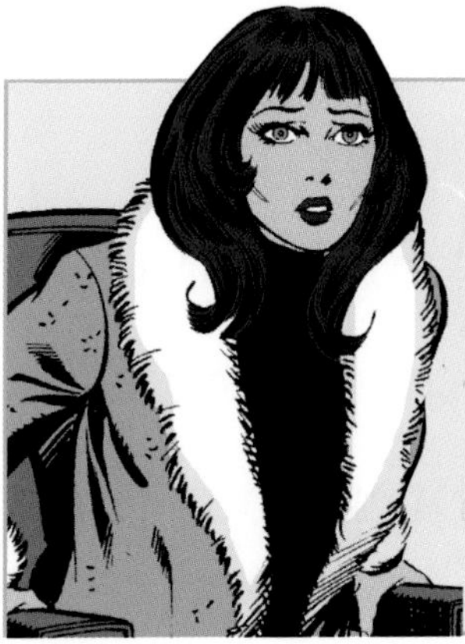

Bethany Cabe

Bethany Cabe is Tony's bodyguard. Like Pepper, she fell in love with Tony. She helped him get better when his health issues became too much for him.

Harold "Happy" Hogan

Harold Hogan is also one of Tony's trusted friends. He is always on hand to offer Tony advice.

Hogan was a professional boxer, but he wasn't very successful. He never smiled because he lost most of his fights! This earned him the ironic nickname "Happy."

One day Tony was driving in a stock-car race when he got into a bad collision. Hogan, who was at the race, acted quickly. He pulled Tony from the blazing wreck and saved his life.

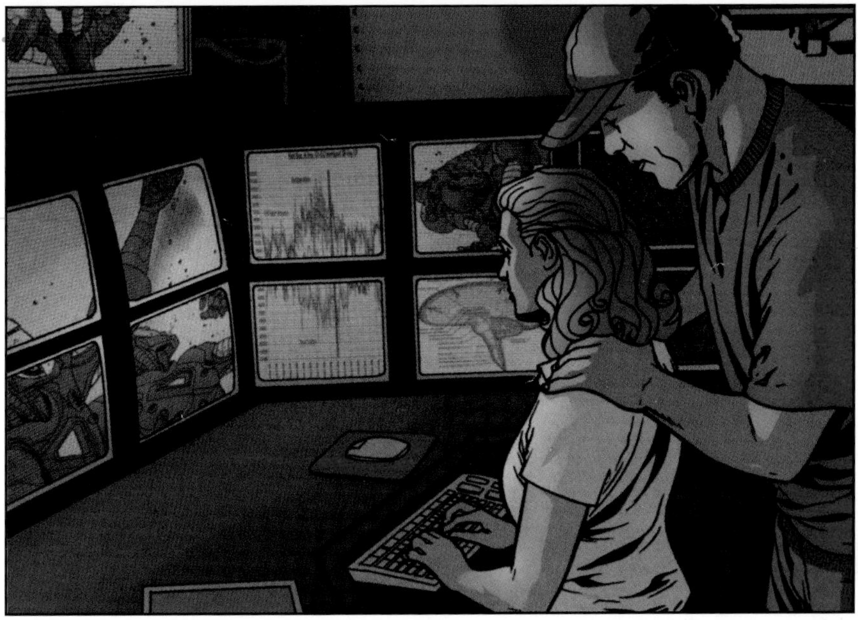

Pepper and Hogan both work for Stark Industries.

Tony was so grateful to Hogan that he hired him to be his chauffeur. Hogan was finally able to stop boxing.

While working at Stark Industries, Hogan fell in love with Pepper Potts. The pair eventually married.

Freak

When Hogan got ill, doctors used Tony's Enervator to save him. However, Hogan was transformed into the monster called Freak.

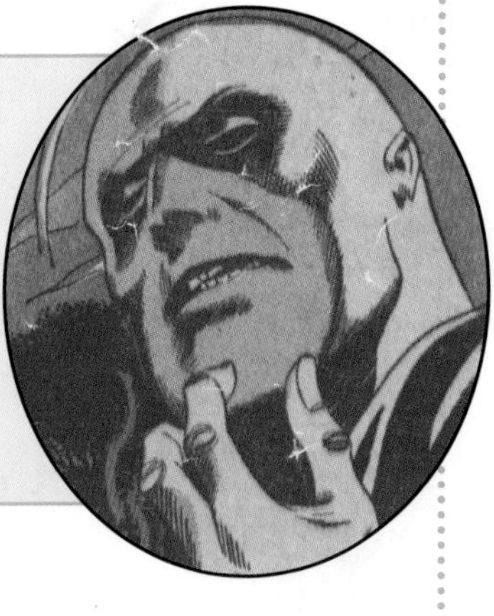

Edwin Jarvis

Edwin Jarvis is Tony's faithful butler. Jarvis earned great honors during World War II as a pilot in the British Royal Air Force. After he left the service, Jarvis went to work as a butler for Tony's parents, Howard and Maria Stark, at their mansion in New York City. Tony inherited the mansion when his parents died. He chose to keep Jarvis on as his butler.

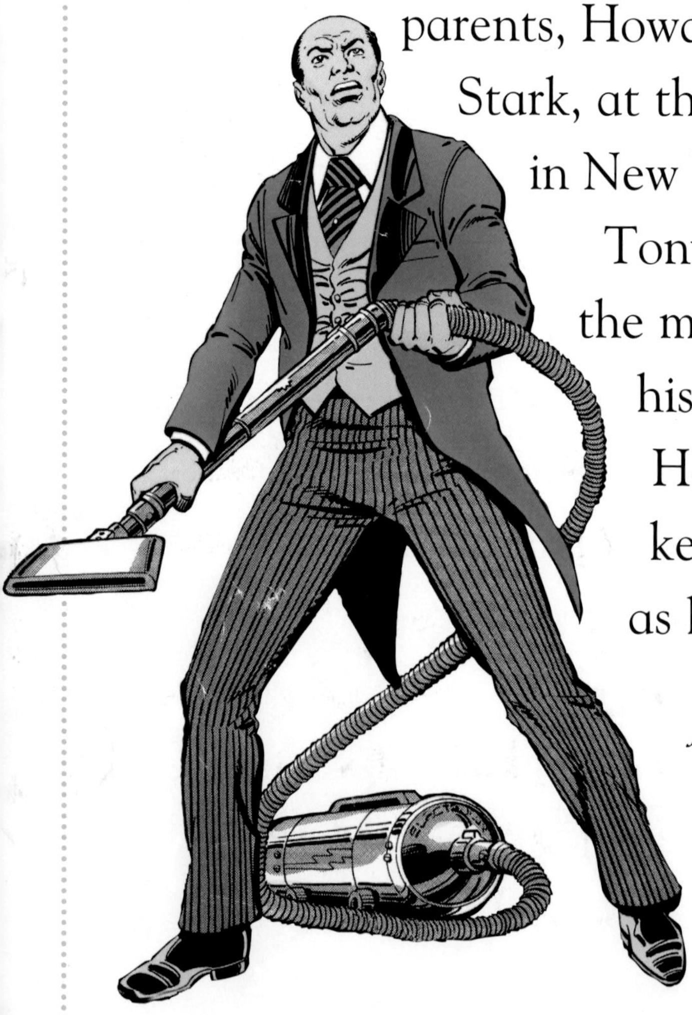

Jarvis uses his trusty vacuum cleaner to tidy the mansion.

Jarvis serves the Avengers their favorite food.

Later, Tony gave the Stark Mansion to the Avengers and it became known as the Avengers Mansion. Jarvis stayed on there as butler and has served the Super Hero team loyally ever since. Jarvis is in charge of all the domestic aspects of the mansion and also looks after the Avengers' financial records.

The Avengers

The Avengers is a Super Hero team that was formed by accident. Loki, the Asgardian God of Evil, wanted revenge on his half-brother, Thor, so he tricked the Hulk into causing a train wreck. Iron Man, Thor, Ant-Man, and Wasp came together to stop his plan. After the group realized Hulk was innocent, they chose to remain a team and Hulk joined them.

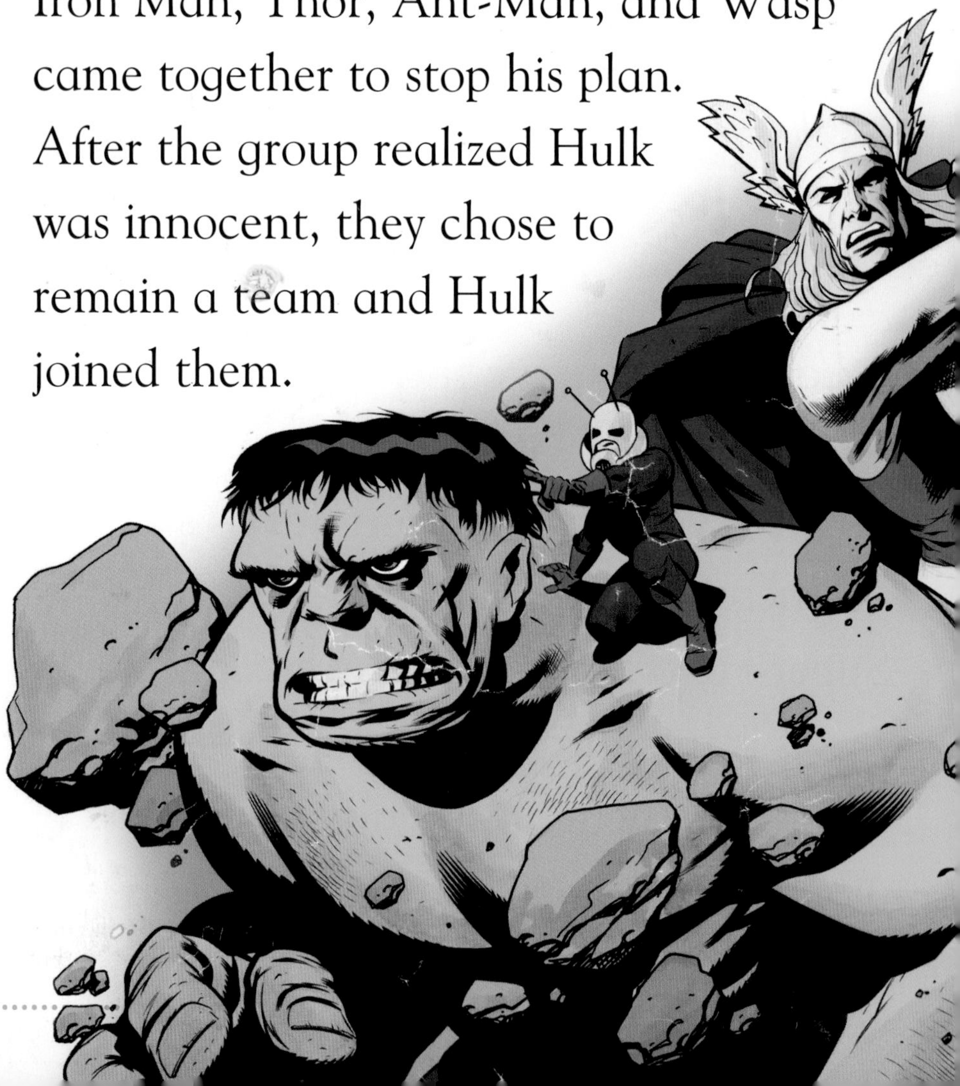

Iron Man has been the Avengers' leader, and Tony gave the group his house to use as their base. He was so loyal to them that they called him the Golden Avenger.

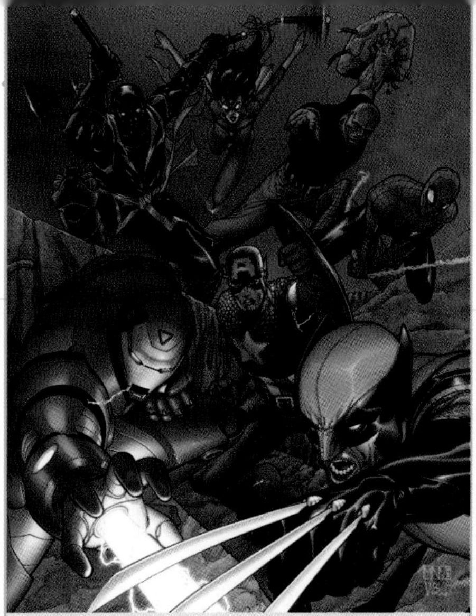

Avenger's role call

Some of the other members of the Avengers include Captain America, She-Hulk, Wonder Man, Scarlet Witch, Vision, Spider-Man, Black Knight, Luke Cage, and Wolverine.

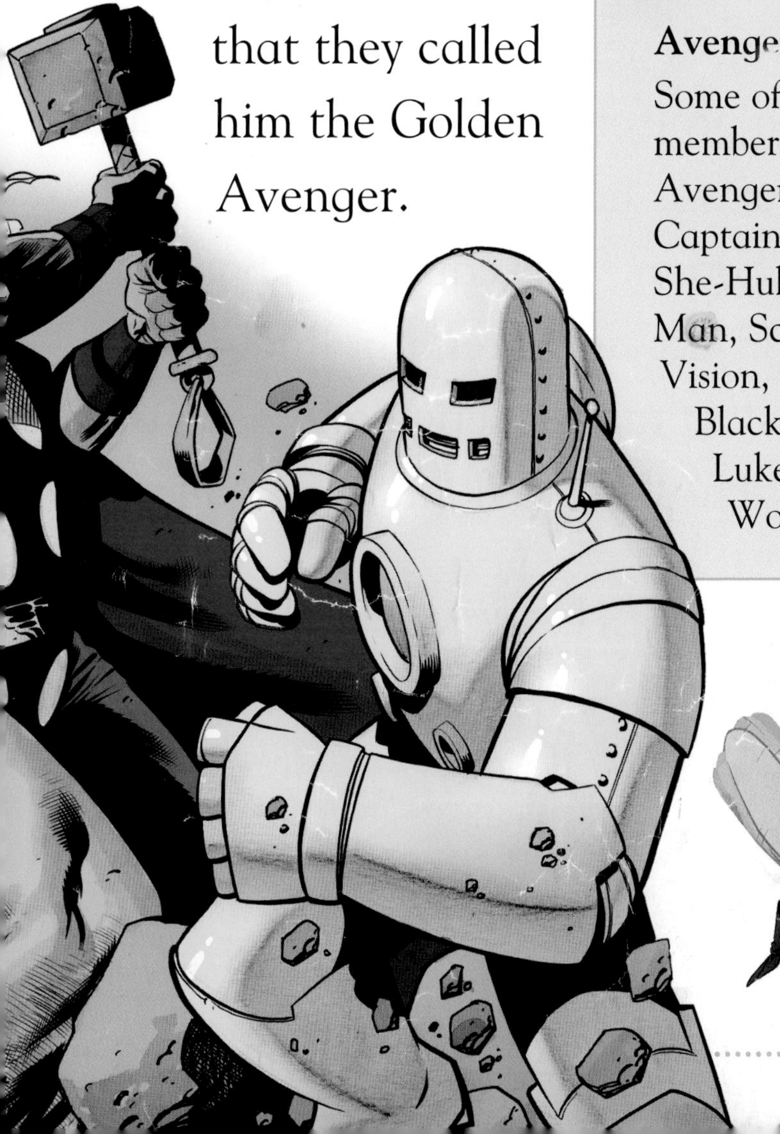

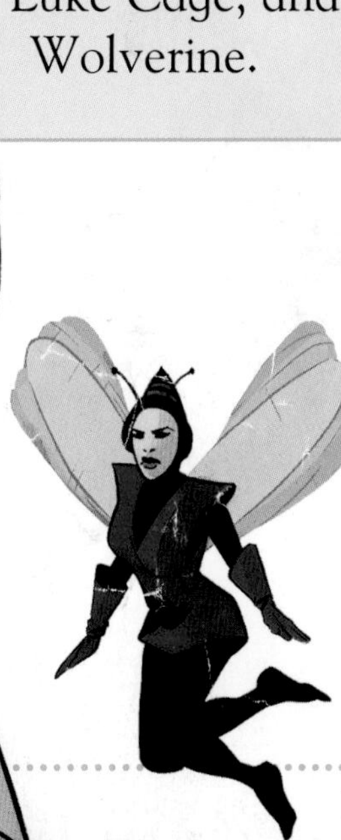

Captain America

Captain America fights alongside Iron Man as a key member of the Avengers.

When World War II began, Steve Rogers wanted to join the army. The army rejected him because he was too weak. So, Rogers took part in a secret research project to create Super Soldiers.

Rogers was injected with a Super Soldier Serum. This caused his body to double in size and strength. Rogers became Captain America and now uses his physical skills to fight Super Villains.

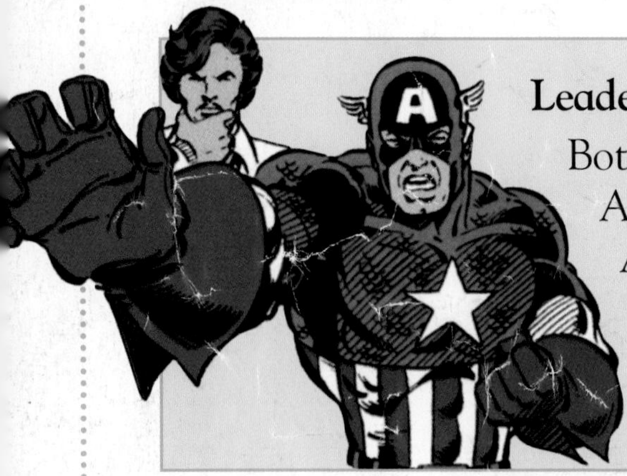

Leaders

Both Iron Man and Captain America have led the Avengers. Cap was also given "founder member" status, when the Hulk left the group.

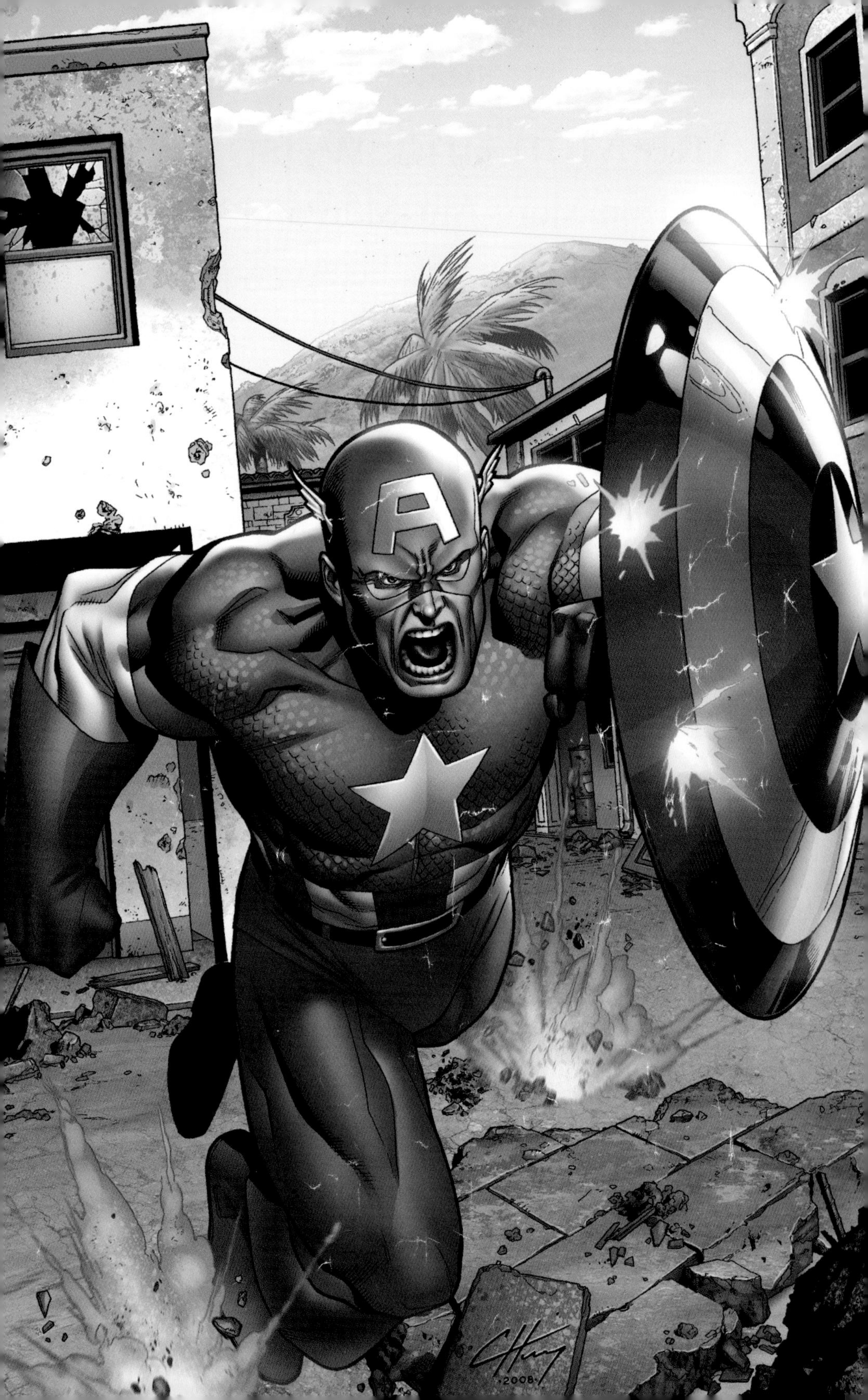
2008

Ant-Man and Wasp

Like Iron Man, Ant-Man and Wasp are original members of the Avengers.

Ant-Man's alter ego is Dr. Henry Pym. Dr. Pym is a scientist who created Pym Particles that shrank him down to the size of an insect. He also made a helmet that allowed him to communicate with insects and fire highly powerful energy blasts.

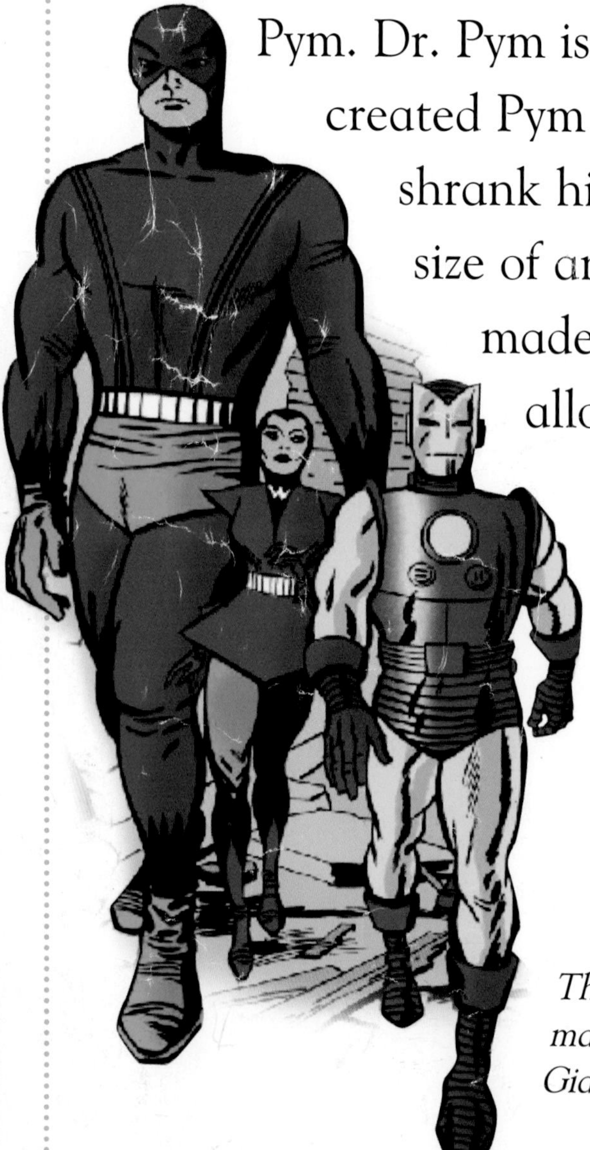

The Pym Particles also made Dr. Pym grow into Giant-Man.

Wasp's alter ego is Janet Van Dyne. Janet fell in love with Pym and they got married.

Ant-Man and Wasp are so small they can fit inside a gun.

Pym used his particles to shrink Janet to insect size, and give her wings and a bio-electric sting.

Ant-Man suggested the Super Heroes become a team and Wasp came up with the name "Avengers."

Ant-Man and Wasp remain two of Iron Man's greatest allies.

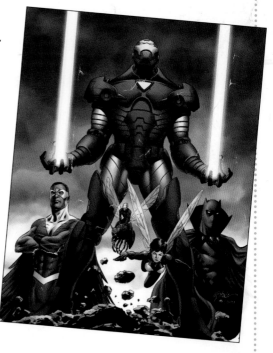

Thor

Thor, the Asgardian God of Thunder, is one of Iron Man's most trusted allies.

Thor was sent to earth by his father, Odin, to learn humility by living among the humans. Thor's jealous half-brother, Loki, took revenge on Thor by forcing him to battle the Hulk. This led to the Avengers being formed. Thor has remained an important member of the Super Hero team.

Thor has great strength and magical abilities, and he uses an unbreakable hammer. This mighty hammer enables him to fly. It also controls storms and opens portals to other dimensions. Thor also wears an enchanted Belt of Strength, which doubles his strength but leaves him weak after he has used it.

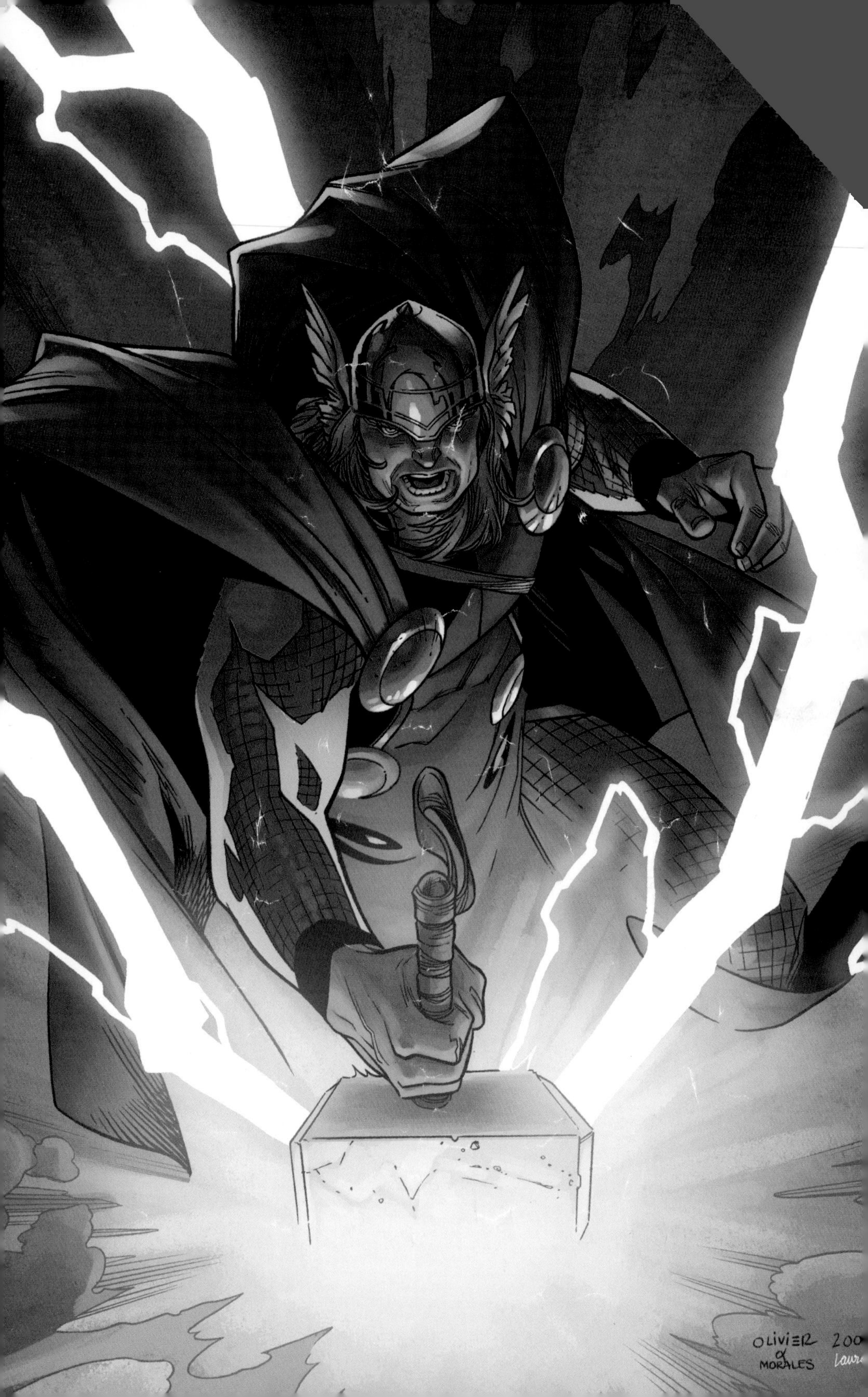
OLIVIER
MORALES

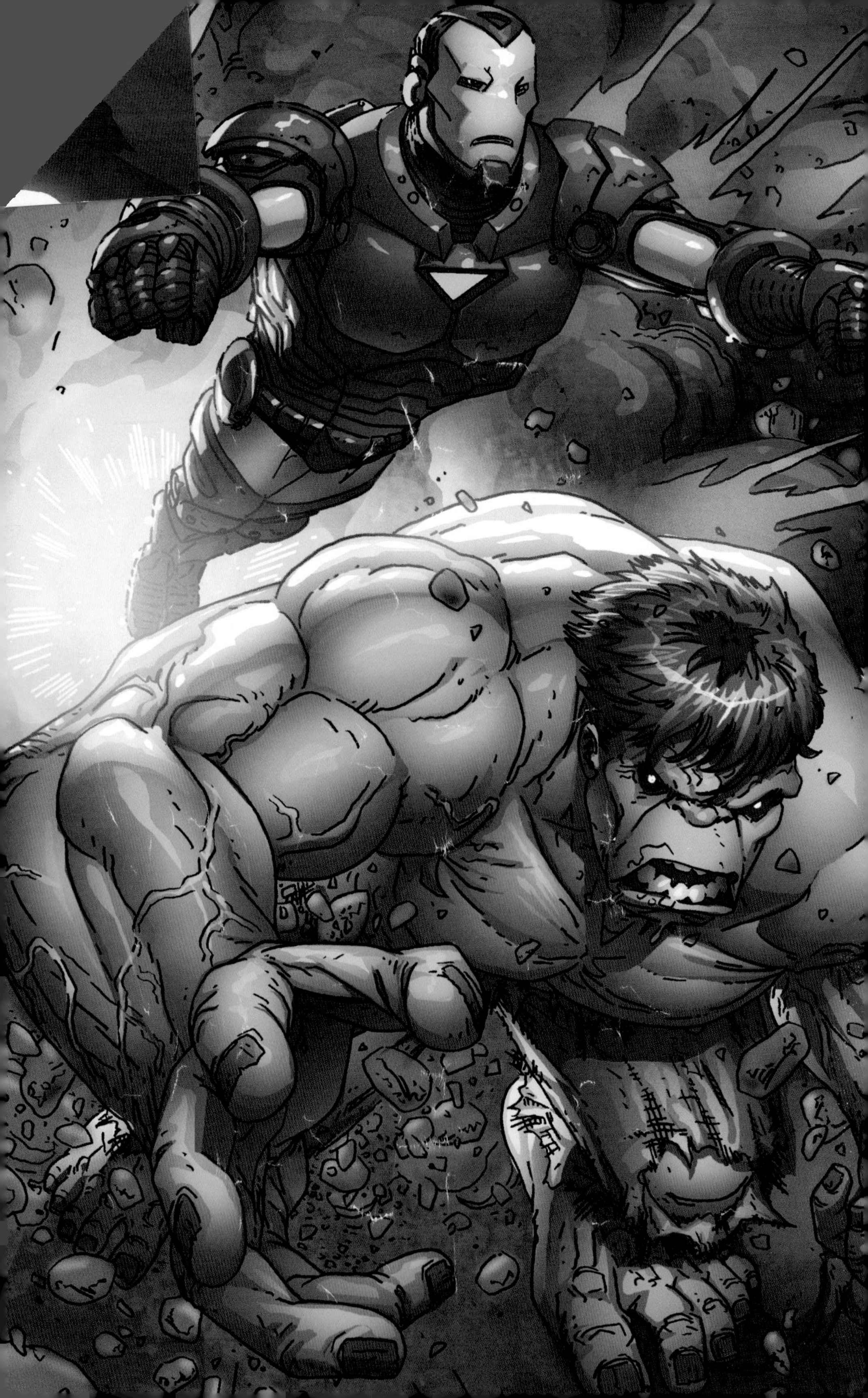

Hulk

The Hulk was a member of the Avengers, but he did not stay in the group for long. However, he still helps Iron Man whenever he is needed.

When Dr. Bruce Banner was caught in a gamma bomb explosion, his body was altered. Now, whenever he gets angry he changes into the green mass of muscle known as the Hulk. He has unlimited strength, and the madder he gets, the stronger he gets.

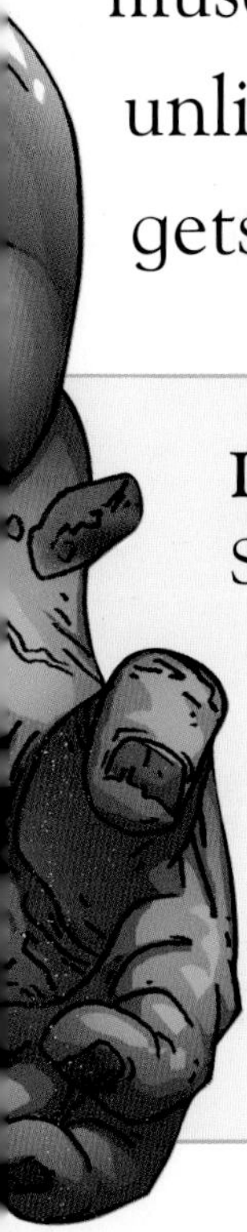

Iron Man's other friends

Some of the other Super Heroes Iron Man has teamed up with are Ka-Zar, Ms. Marvel, Daredevil, the Fantastic Four, and Spider-Man.

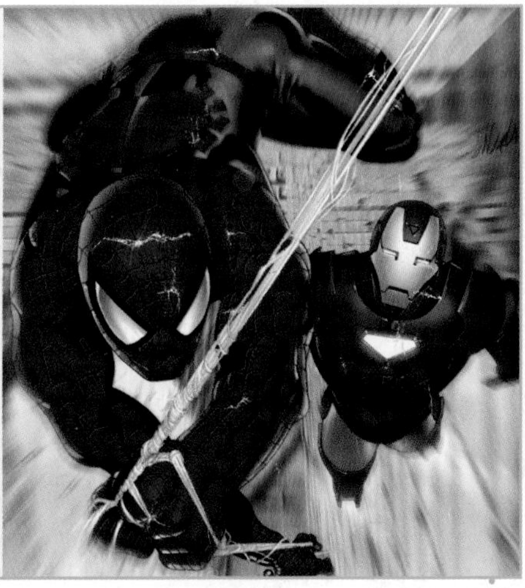

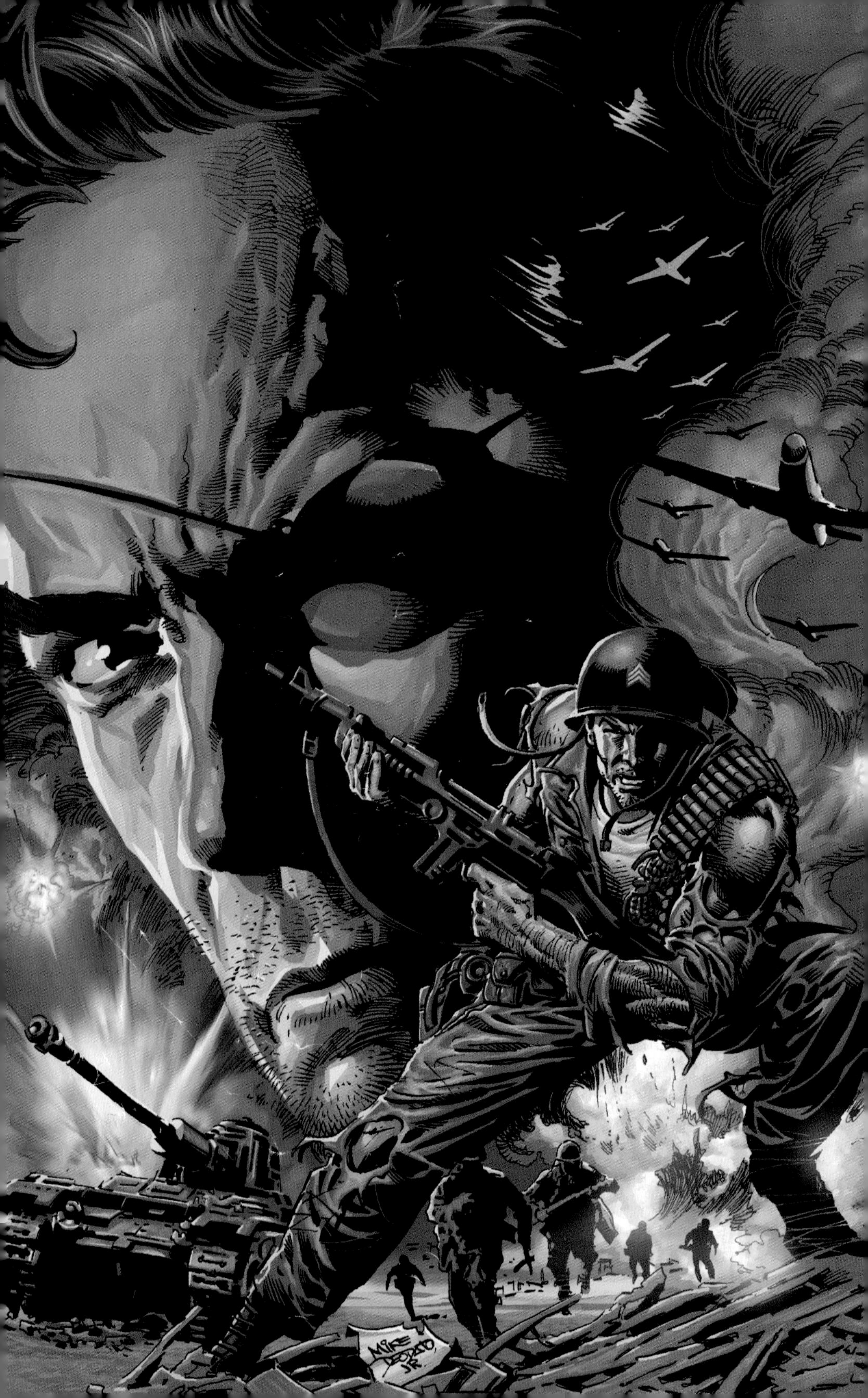
MIKE DEODATO JR.

Nick Fury and S.H.I.E.L.D.

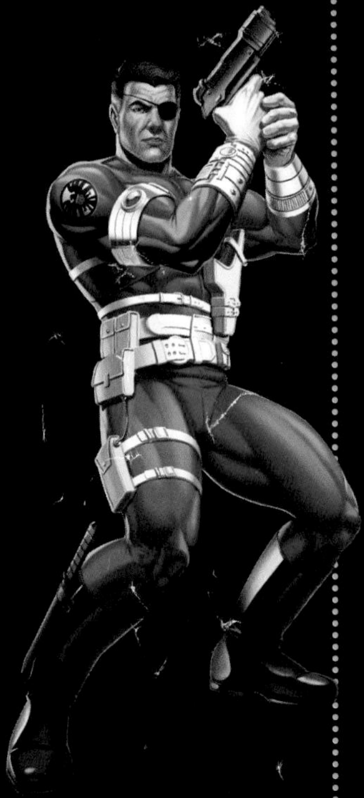

Nick Fury has worked closely with Iron Man as director of the worldwide anti-terrorism organization called S.H.I.E.L.D. Its name stands for Supreme Headquarters International Espionage Law-enforcement Division.

Fury was born in a tough neighborhood in New York City. He joined the army during World War II. Later, he became the leader of the Howling Commandos, a combat unit who take on dangerous missions.

Fury was made the liaison between the government and the Super Heroes. He became the director of S.H.I.E.L.D. when Iron Man recruited him.

Obadiah Stane

Iron Man has fought many enemies during his life. One of his main enemies is Obadiah Stane.

Stane is a ruthless businessman. He took control of Stark Industries and left Tony homeless. Stane has battled Iron Man, while wearing an armored battlesuit and calling himself Iron Monger. Eventually Iron Man defeated Iron Monger.

Like father, like son
Obadiah Stane's son is also Iron Man's enemy. Ezekiel Stane battled Iron Man as a superhuman cyborg. Ezekiel can generate as much energy as Iron Man.

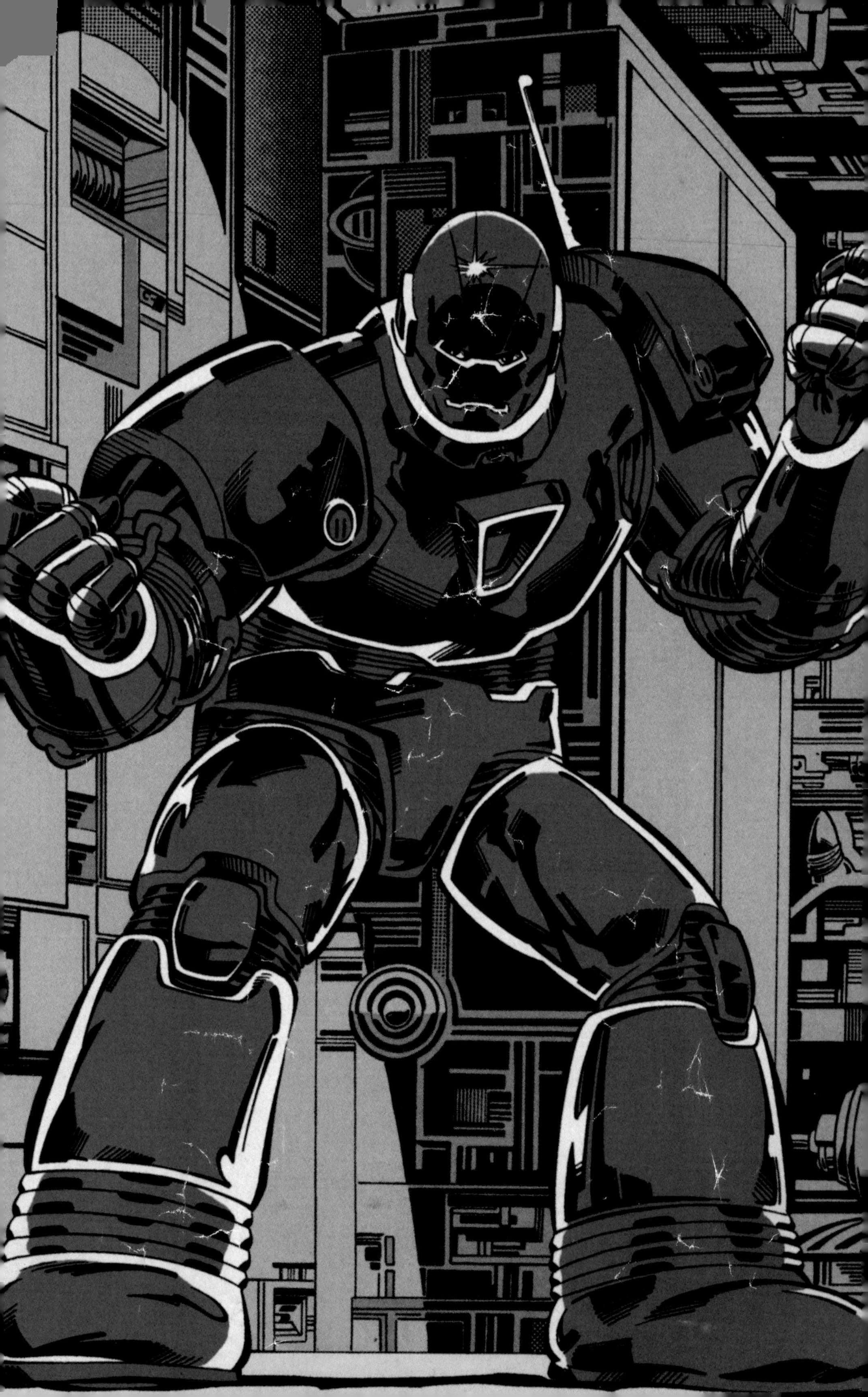

Justin Hammer

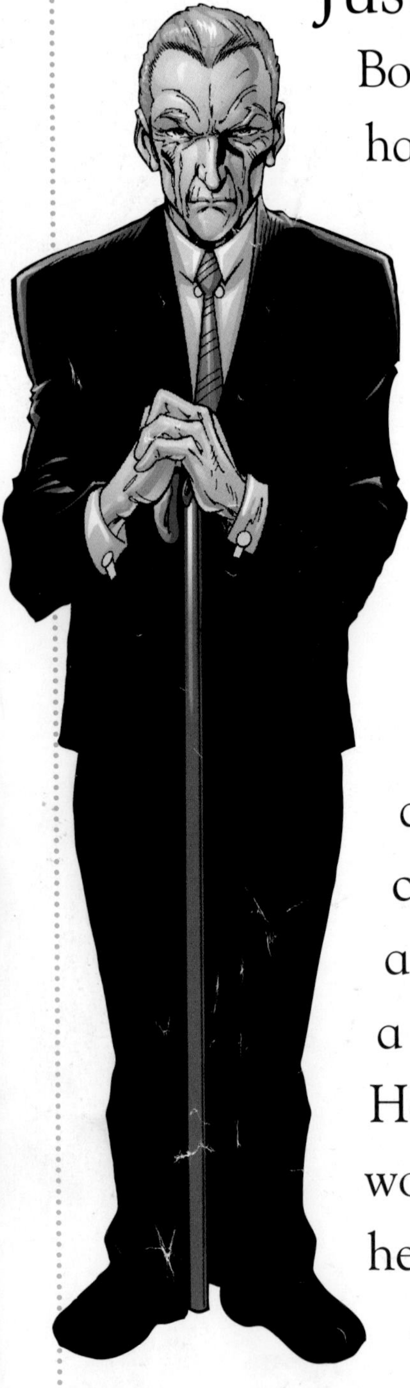

Both Tony and Iron Man have to face enemies. Justin Hammer is one of Tony's business competitors. He tried to destroy Tony using Iron Man. Hammer was a financial genius who wanted to take over Stark Industries. He used a hypersonic device to take control of the Iron Man armor, then used it to kill a foreign ambassador. Hammer hoped that Tony would be blamed and that he could then take control of Stark Industries.

Hammer's help

Some of the Super Villains Hammer has hired to fight Tony and Iron Man include Whiplash, Spymaster, Man-Killer, Blizzard, Boomerang, and Water Wizard.

When Tony cleared his name, Hammer went into hiding. Later, he began secretly giving money to various Super Villains to help him battle against both Tony and Iron Man.

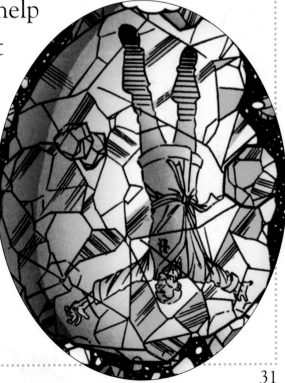

Hammer was trapped in a block of ice in space when his space station exploded.

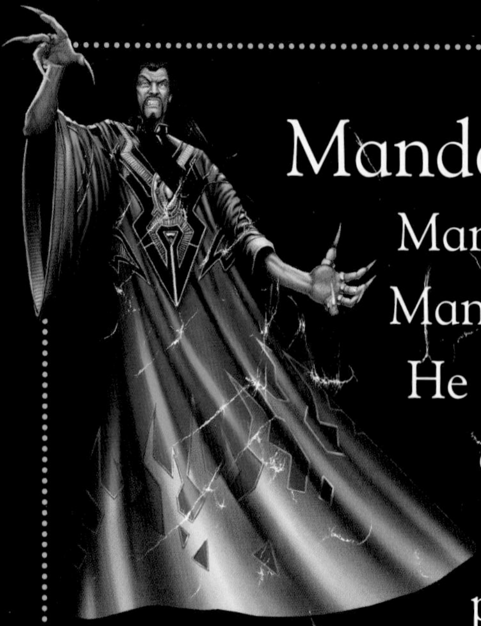

Mandarin

Mandarin is one of Iron Man's most deadly foes. He is a martial arts master and scientific genius.

During a quest for power, Mandarin entered the forbidden Valley of Spirits. He found the wreck of an alien starship there. The ship contained the Ten Rings of Power that Mandarin now wears.

Mandarin is the only one who can use the ten rings. They allow him to control someone else's mind, rearrange matter, and create fire, ice, electricity, and blinding bursts of light. Mandarin has used these powers to try to take control of the world. Each time, Iron Man and the Avengers have stopped him.

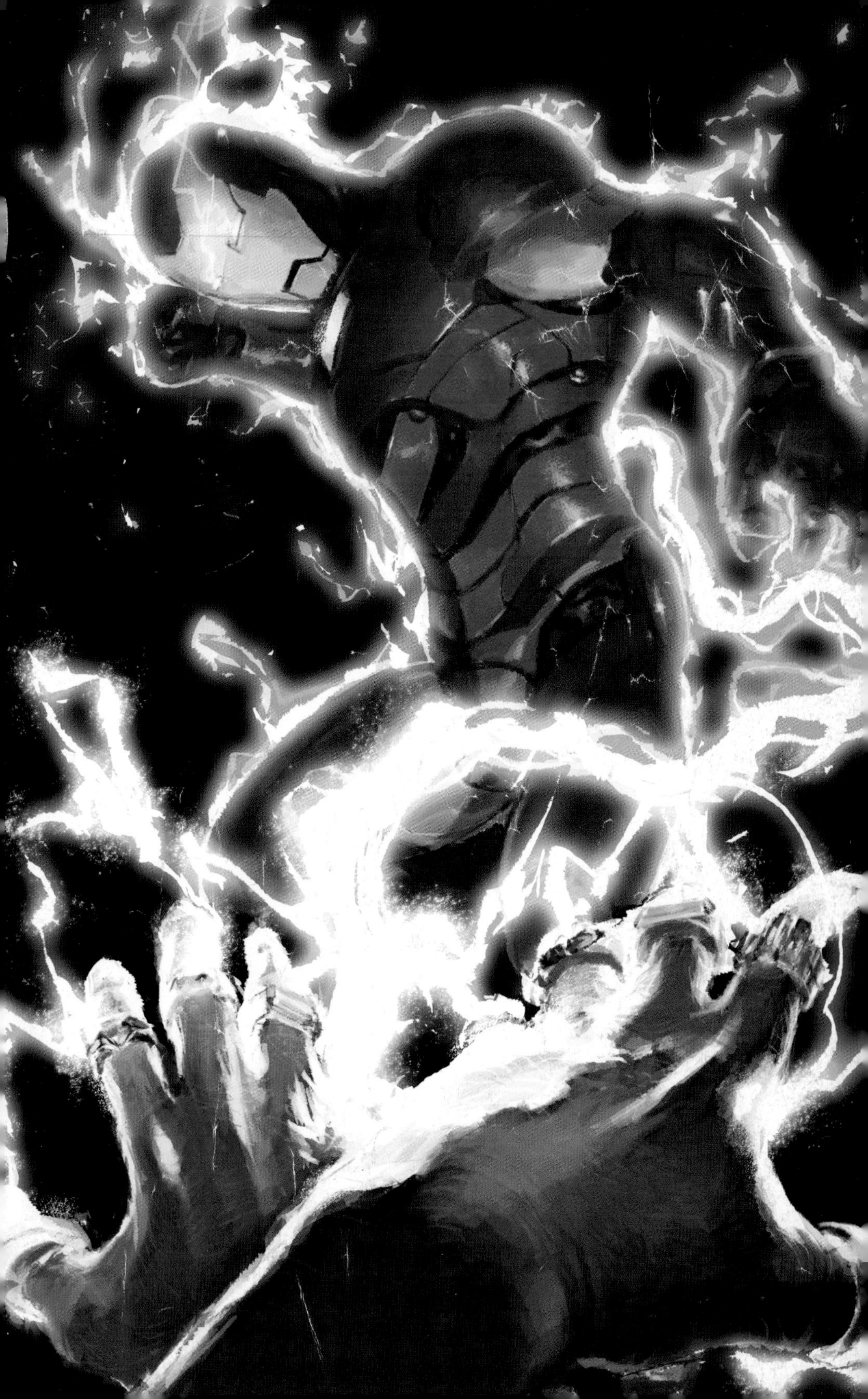

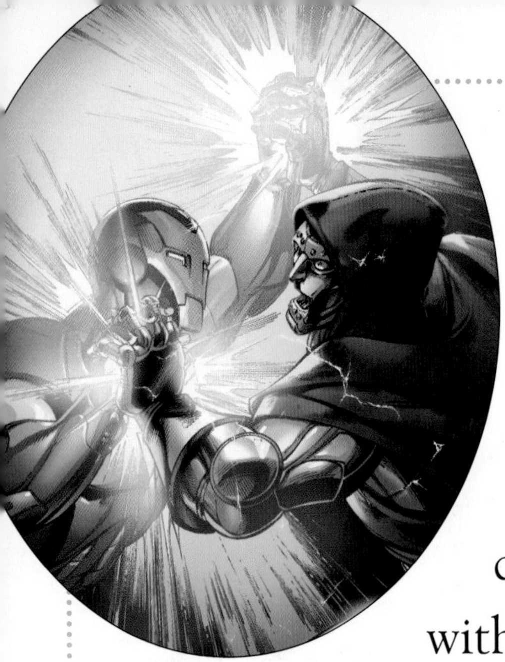

Doctor Doom

Doctor Doom is the greatest enemy of the Fantastic Four. However, Doom has also come into conflict with Iron Man and his fellow Avengers many times.

Victor von Doom was born in the tiny kingdom of Latveria. He scarred his face in an explosion when one of his experiments went badly wrong. Doom wears a mask to hide his features.

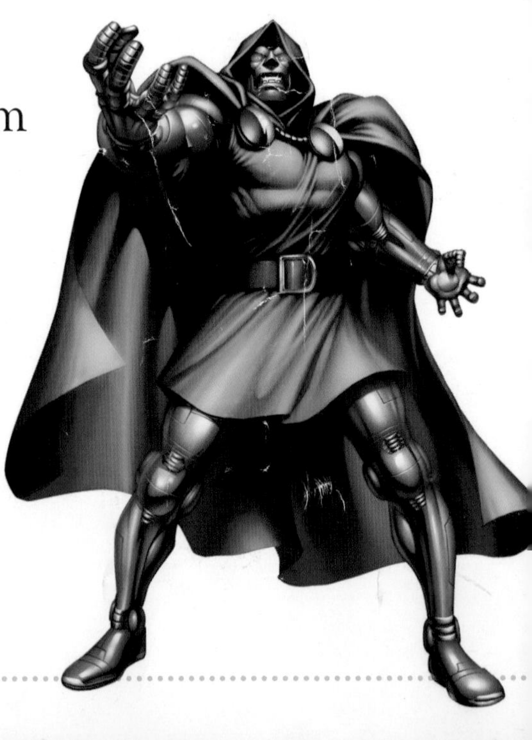

Victor would not listen to people who tried to tell him his experiment would go wrong.

Doomquest
Iron Man fought with Doctor Doom, when Iron Man attacked Doom's castle. Doom's Time Platform sent the pair back to King Arthur's time, before Iron Man or Doom were even born!

Doom also began wearing an armored battlesuit, which he built using his scientific knowledge. The battlesuit gives him superhuman strength and is filled with weapons. If anyone tries to touch the suit, they receive an electric shock.

Doctor Doom also has a vast knowledge of sorcery and can transfer his consciousness into the body of another person.

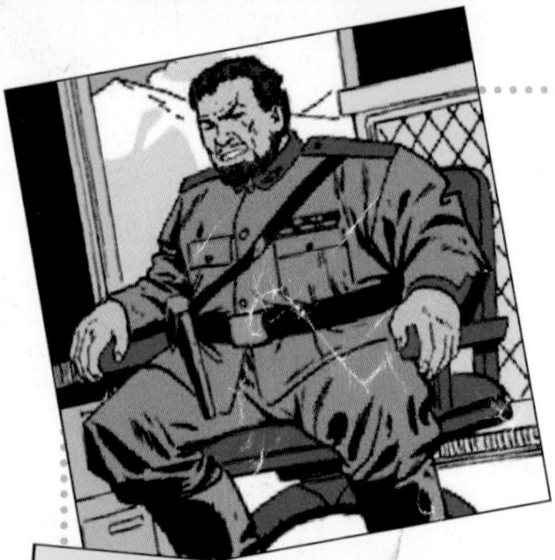

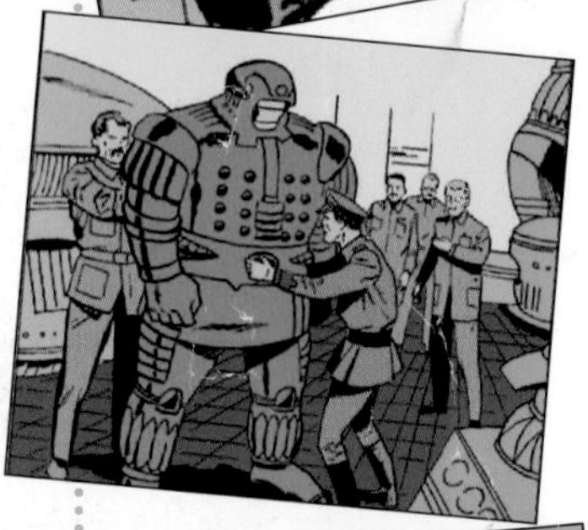

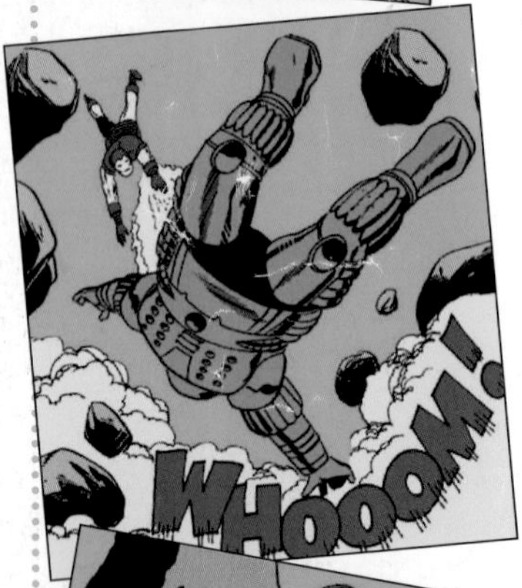
WHOOOM!

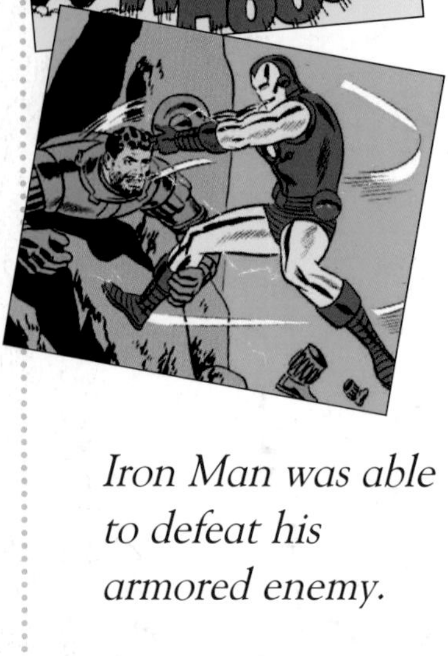

Iron Man was able to defeat his armored enemy.

Titanium Man

A number of Iron Man's most dangerous enemies have also used technology created by Tony to make their own armor.

Titanium Man's alter ego is a Russian inventor named Boris Bullski. Bullski made the Titanium Man armor so that he could defeat Iron Man.

Like Iron Man's armor, Titanium Man's battlesuit increases his strength, allows him to fly, protects him from harm, and enables him to fire energy blasts.

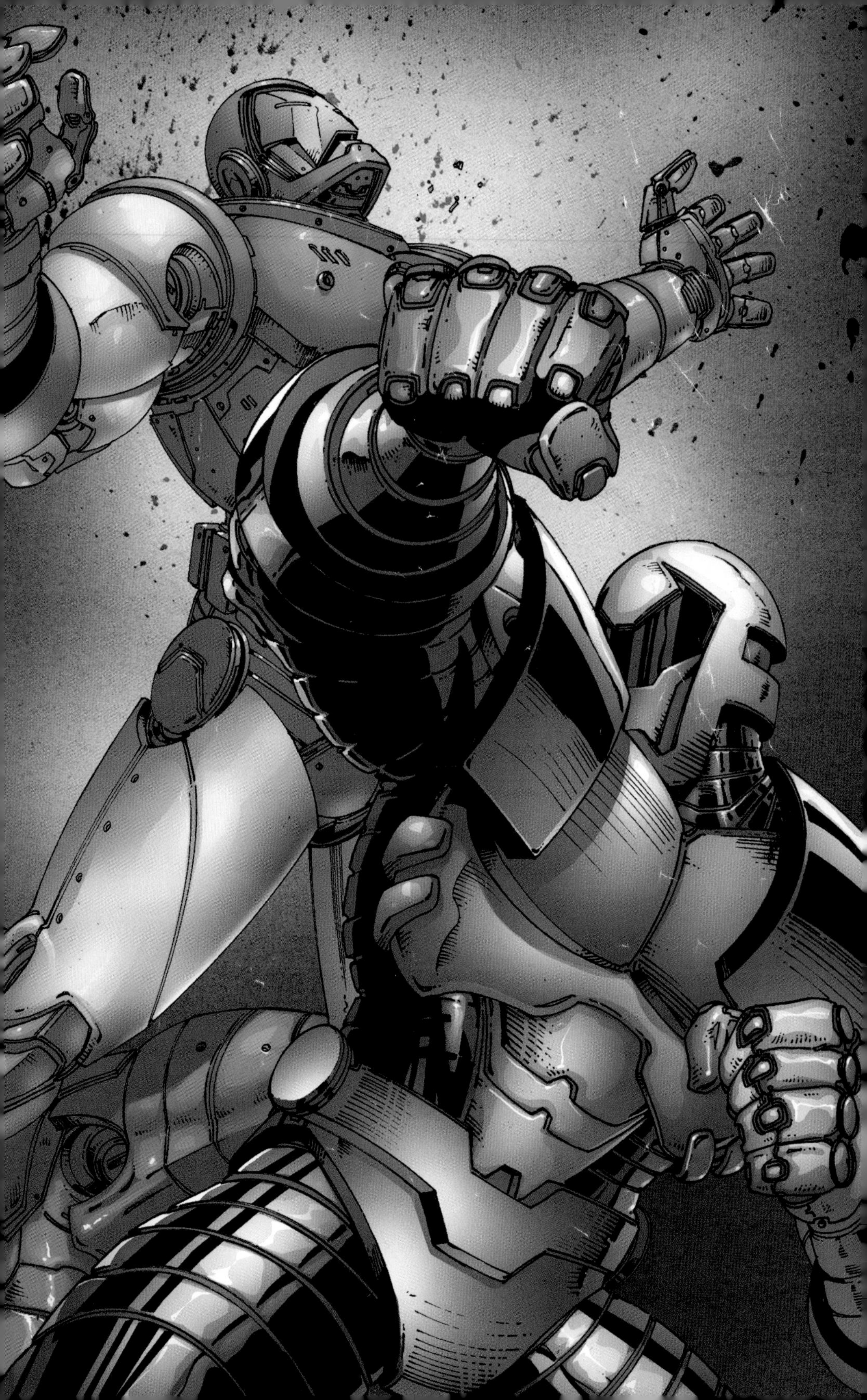

Even though Ultimo is big, it can run quickly.

Ultimo

Ultimo is a giant robot who has fought Iron Man many times. It was created by aliens and programmed to destroy anything in its path.

When Ultimo was chasing beings from the planet Rajak, it crashed onto Earth. Mandarin, one of Iron Man's enemies, found Ultimo. He reprogrammed the robot to do anything he wanted it to.

Iron Man and his friends have tried to destroy Ultimo several times. Once, Iron Man trapped the evil robot beneath the Earth's crust. Another time, James Rhodes gathered several of Tony's trusted friends together.

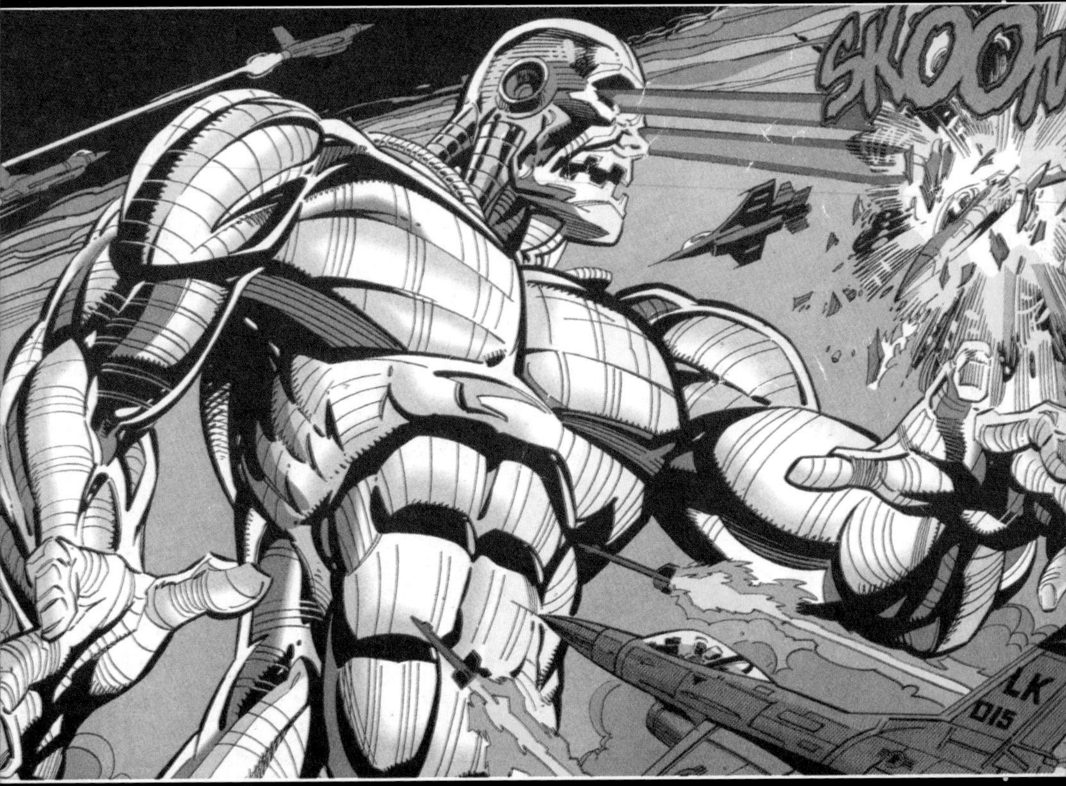
SKOOM
LK
D15

Ultimo can fire powerful giant beams from its eyes that can disintegrate anything they hit.

They included Harold Hogan and Bethany Cabe. The group put on old Iron Man armor and formed the Iron Legion, but they could not stop Ultimo. Finally, Iron Man placed a device onto Ultimo that caused lightning to strike him, shutting him down.

Crimson Dynamo

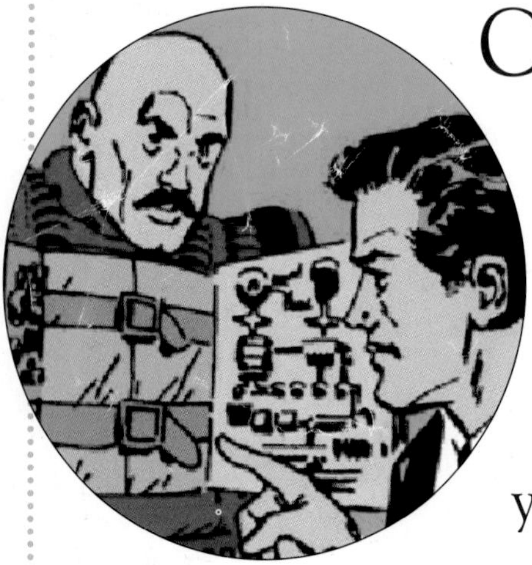

The Crimson Dynamo wears a battlesuit that is very similar to Iron Man's armor. Over the years, six men have worn the suit, but none of them have defeated Iron Man.

Anton Vanko invented the suit and wore it to fight Iron Man. Later, he went to work for Tony as a scientist.

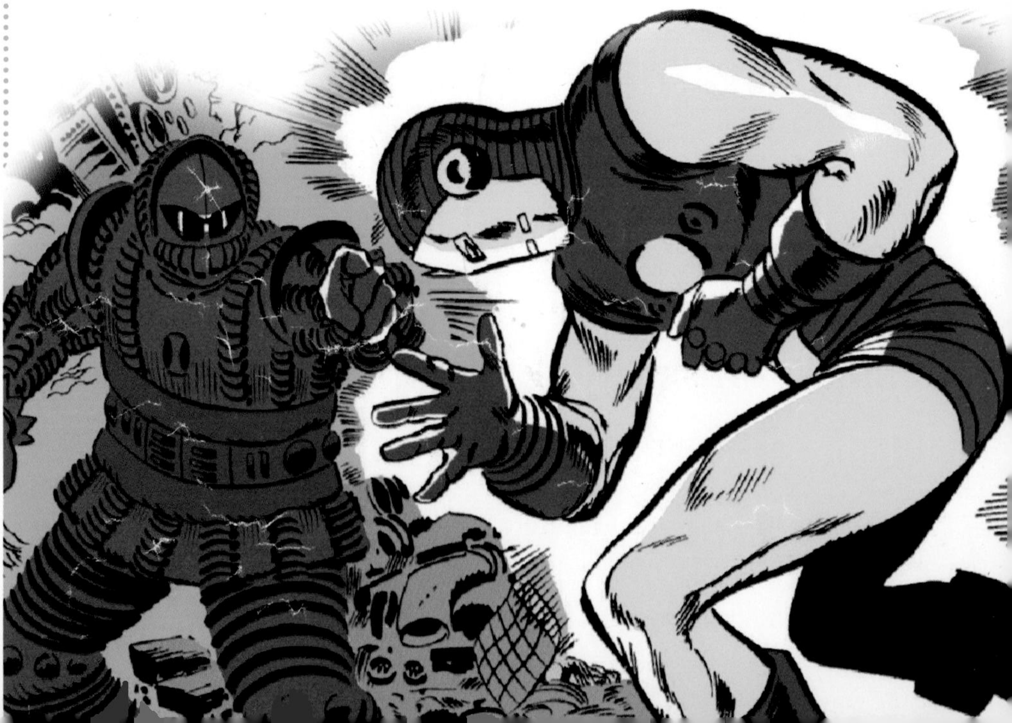

The Crimson Dynamo's armored battlesuit gives superstrength to anyone who wears it.

To begin with, Valentin Shatalov also battled Iron Man as the Crimson Dynamo. However, he later changed sides and teamed up with Iron Man. The duo defeated the armored Super Villain Titanium Man.

The Crimson Dynamo's battlesuit gives its wearer the ability to fly and protects the wearer from attack.

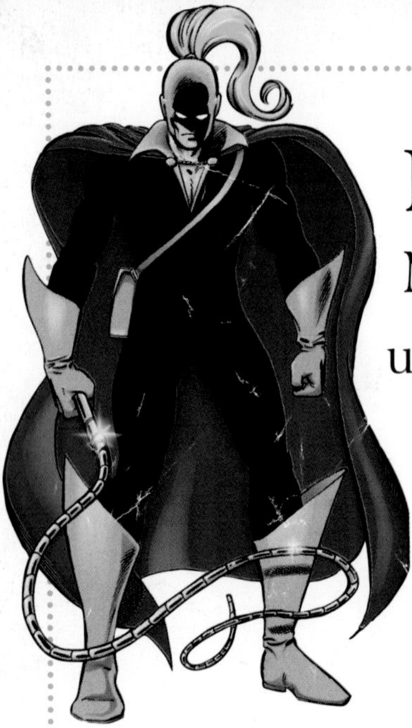

Backlash

Mark Scarlotti was a top undercover agent in a crime group called the Maggia. Before Scarlotti became Backlash, he was known as Whiplash. He wore a battlesuit made of steel mesh and a bulletproof cape. Whiplash was expert at using a whip as a weapon and brilliant at hand-to-hand combat and martial arts. On one occasion, he battled Iron Man to a draw.

Later, Scarlotti was hired by Justin Hammer to join a group of costumed criminals. Hammer bought Scarlotti new weapons and armor, and he became Backlash. Once again he fought Iron Man, but this time Iron Man won.

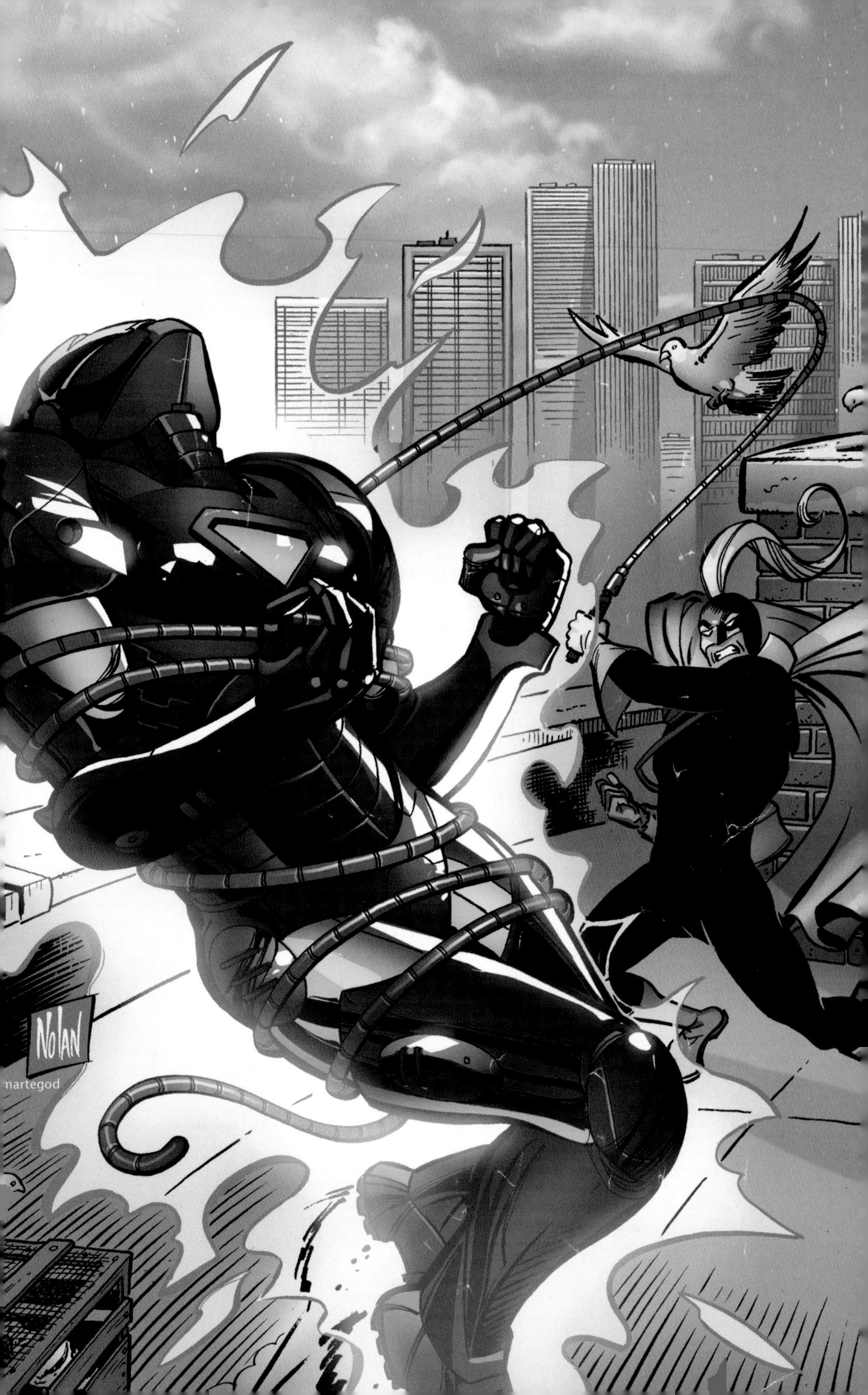
NOLAN
martegod

Spymaster

Spymaster is an industrial spy who has tried to steal technological secrets from Stark Industries many times. His true identity is unknown. Spymaster works with a team called the Espionage Elite to battle Iron Man. Iron Man has always stopped the group. Spymaster is a master of disguise and has a hoverjet that allows him to fly. Once, Spymaster stole the detailed plans for Iron Man's armor.

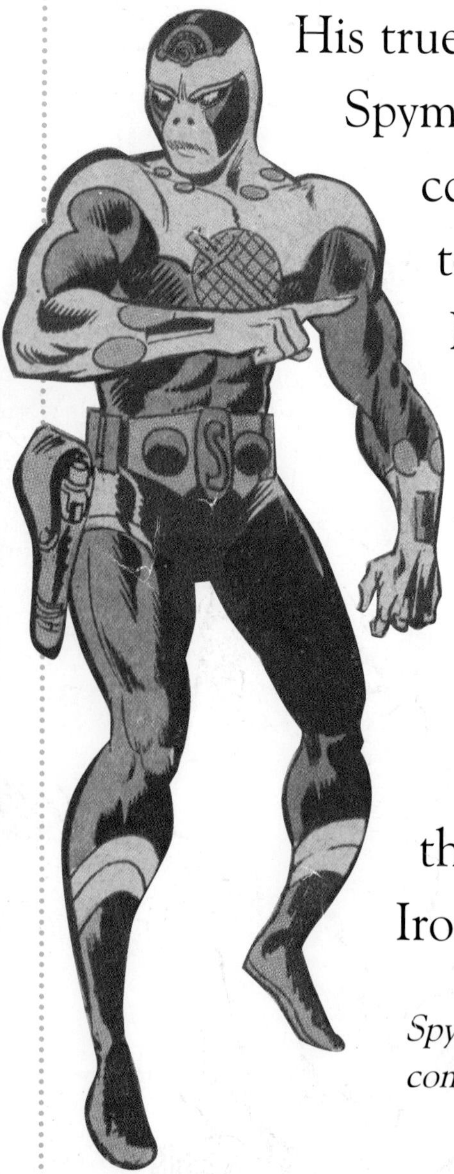

Spymaster's suit is completely bulletproof.

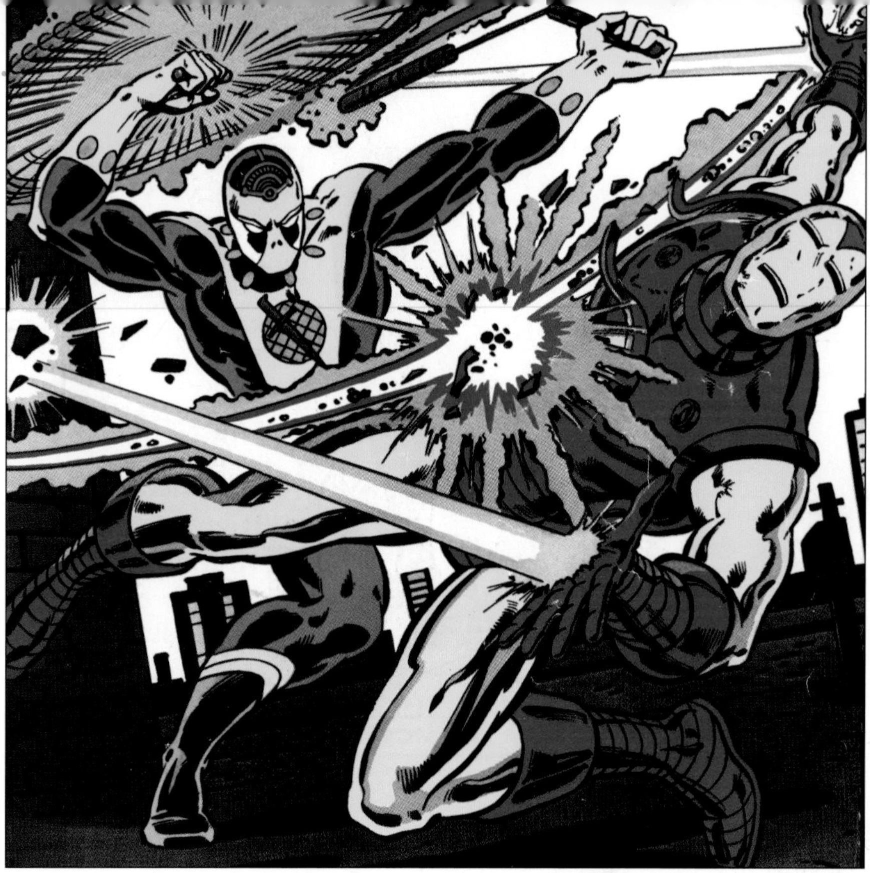

Spymaster is skilled at hand-to-hand combat.

Using these, he created a group of agents called the Guardsmen. They wore suits as powerful as Iron Man's and often fought him.

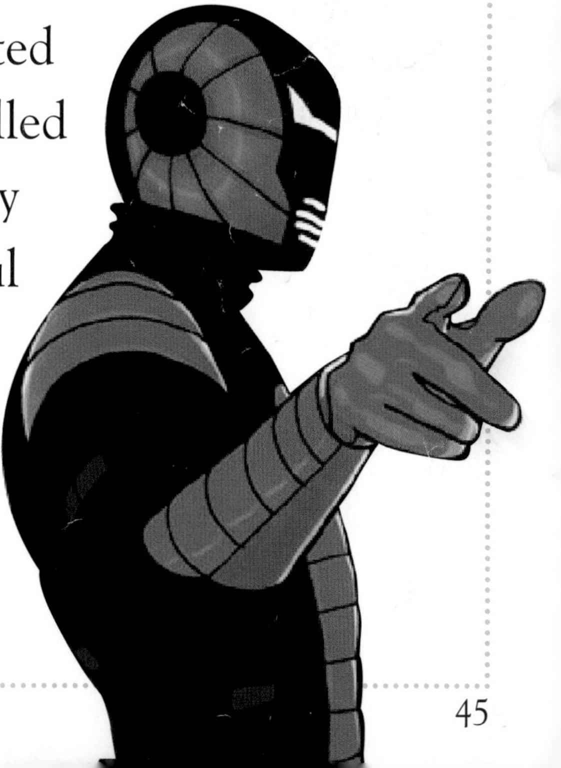

The latest Spymaster wears a red and black suit.

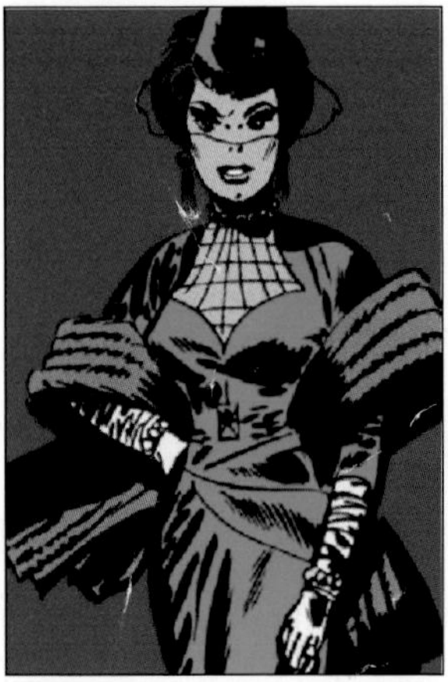

Black Widow

Natasha Romanova is a Russian spy. She was given the code name "Black Widow," and was sent to America to spy on Stark Industries. She hoped to steal Tony's military and technological secrets for the Russian government.

During these missions, Black Widow met Hawkeye, a member of the Avengers. Hawkeye convinced Black Widow to change sides. She joined Iron Man in the Avengers and even served as the leader of the team.

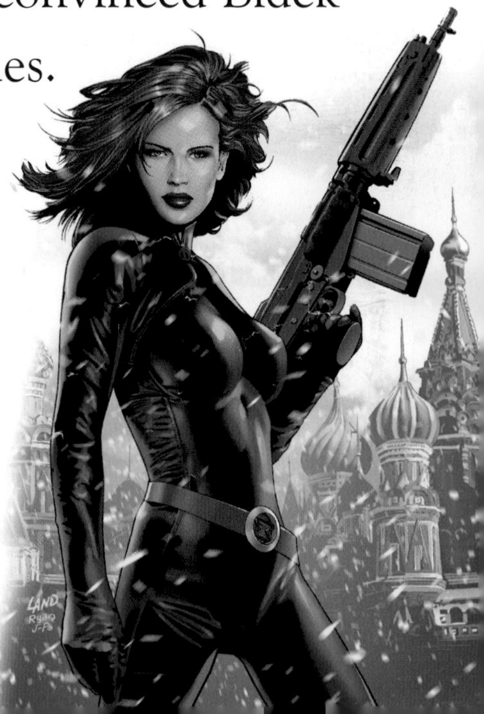

Black Widow has also been a S.H.I.E.L.D. member.

Iron Man's other enemies

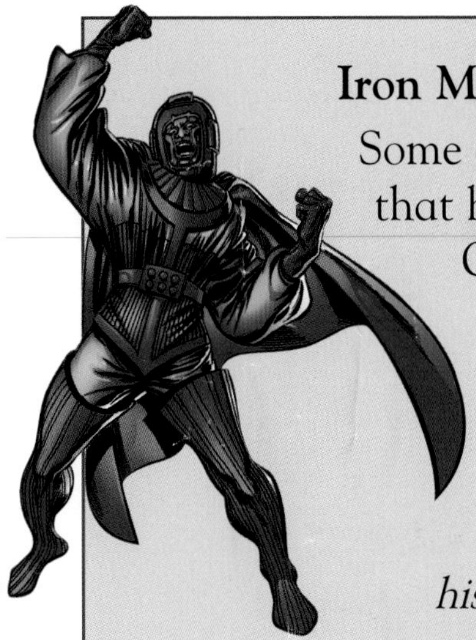

Some of Iron Man's other enemies that he has battled include Kang the Conqueror, Melter, Fin Fang Foom, and MODOK.

Kang the Conqueror's advanced battlesuit increases his strength against his enemies.

Melter has fought Iron Man, and his alter ego, Bruno Horgan, is Tony's business competitor.

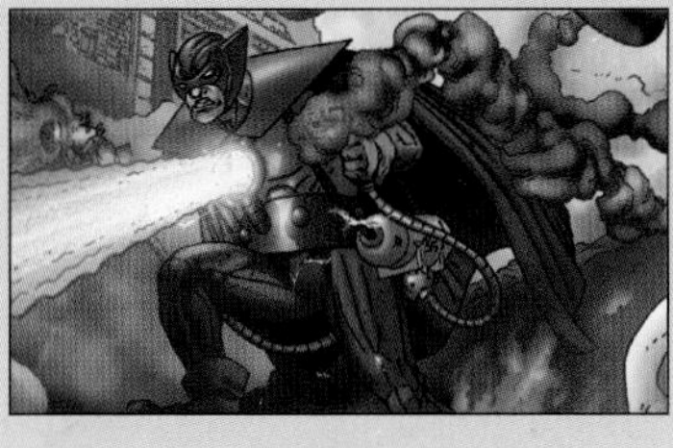

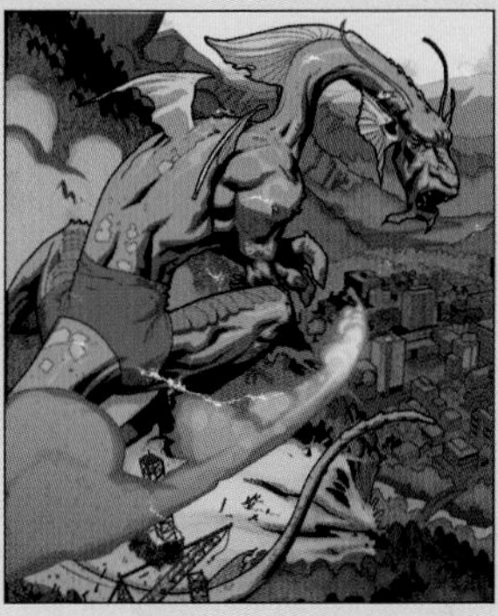

Fin Fang Foom is a fire-breathing alien who is several centuries old.

MODOK stands for Mental Organism Designed Only for Killing. MODOK has a brain like a computer.

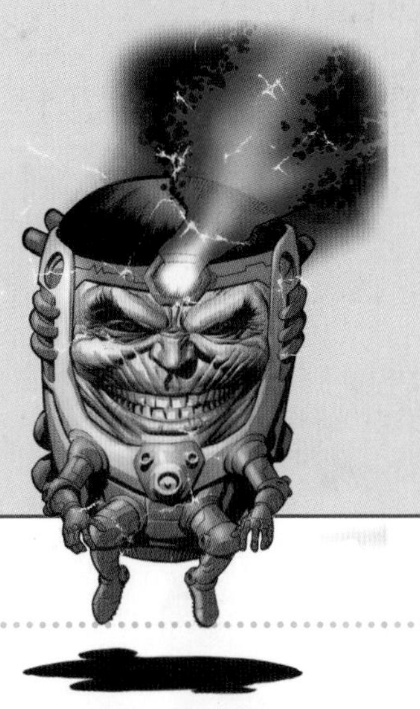

Glossary

accounting
Keeping financial records.

alter ego
The opposite side of a person.

ambassador
A person who represents a country.

aviation
To do with flying airplanes.

butler
A male servant who takes care of all the needs of a household.

chauffeur
A person employed to drive a car.

collision
A crash.

competitors
People in the same business who are in competition with each other.

consciousness
A person's mind.

decorated
Given awards, medals, or honors.

domestic
To do with the household.

espionage
To do with spying.

eventually
In the end.

framed
Blamed for something you did not do.

generate
To produce.

humility
Modesty.

hypersonic
To do with fast signals carried by sound waves.

inherited
Received something from a relation after his or her death.

ironic
A word or phrase that expresses the opposite of what is meant.

liaison
A connection between people or groups.

mansion
A very large house.

pinpoint
Very focused.

portal
A doorway.

project
To shoot out.

repulsor
Something that forces a thing back.

sorcery
Magical powers.

stock-car race
A race using cars that are similar to passenger cars.

technology
Scientific methods.

Index